SHATTERED

Paul
Langan

Scor

BLUFORD SERIES TP

Praise for the Bluford Series:

"Once I started reading, I couldn't sleep. My hands were sweating and my heart was pumping. I thought something was wrong with me. These books are *that* exciting."

— *Kareem S.*

"I love the Bluford Series because I can relate to the stories and the characters. They are just like real life. Ever since I read the first one, I've been hooked."

— *Jolene P.*

"On a scale of 1–10, the scale breaks if I rate the Bluford Series. They are *that* good!"

— *Cornell C.*

"The last thing I wanted to do was read a Bluford book or any book. But after a few pages, I couldn't put the book down. I felt like I was a witness in the story, like I was inside it."

— *Ray F.*

"I found it very easy to lose myself in these books. They kept my interest from beginning to end and were always realistic. The characters are vivid, and the endings left me in eager anticipation of the next book."

— *Keziah J.*

"Man! These books are amazing!"

— *Dominique J.*

"Usually I don't like to read, but I couldn't put the Bluford books down. They kept me interested from beginning to end."

—*Jesus B.*

"My school is just like Bluford High. The characters are just like people I know. These books are real!"

—*Jessica K.*

"I thought the Bluford Series was going to be boring, but once I started, I couldn't stop reading. I had to keep going just to see what would happen next. I have to admit I enjoyed myself. Now I'm done, and I can't wait for more books."

—*Jamal C.*

"All the Bluford books are great. There wasn't one that I didn't like, and I read them all—twice!"

— *Sequoyah D.*

"I've been reading these books for the last three days and can't get them out of my mind. They are *that* good!"

—*Stephen B.*

"Each Bluford book gives you a story that could happen to anyone. The details make you feel like you are inside the books. The storylines are amazing and realistic. I loved them all."

—*Elpiclio B.*

"All my friends and I agree. The Bluford Series is bangin'."

—*Margarita R.*

Shattered

Paul Langan

Series Editor: Paul Langan

TOWNSEND PRESS
www.townsendpress.com

Books in the Bluford Series

Copyright © 2007 by Townsend Press, Inc.
Printed in the United States of America

9 8 7 6 5 4 3 2 1

Townsend Press, Inc.
1038 Industrial Drive
West Berlin, New Jersey 08091
www.townsendpress.com

ISBN-13: 978-1-59194-069-2
ISBN-10: 1-59194-069-9
Library of Congress Control Number:
2006922149

Chapter 1

"Girl, where you at?"

Darcy Wills winced at the voice blasting through her new cell phone. It was her best friend, Tarah Carson, and she sounded angry.

"C'mon, Darce. You're late," Tarah scolded.

Darcy knew Tarah was right even before she looked at her watch. She should have left the house ten minutes ago. Instead she was staring at her reflection in the bathroom mirror, hoping Hakeem Randall wouldn't notice the guilt in her eyes or the worry that haunted her face. So much had changed in the few months since they'd broken up. *Too much*, Darcy thought.

"I'm sorry, Tarah. It's just that—"

"Tell her I'm starvin'," yelled Cooper

Hodden, Tarah's boyfriend, in the background. "Tell her if she don't get here soon, I'ma start eatin' without her."

His voice was so loud Darcy held the cell phone away from her ear. It sounded like he and Tarah were in the hallway, not several blocks away at Niko's Pizza.

"Stop talkin' nonsense, Coop," Tarah replied. "We ain't eatin' nothin' till she gets here."

"C'mon, Tar! Why you gotsta be that way?" Cooper complained. "Don't ya hear my stomach growlin'?"

"Hold on one second, girl," Tarah said.

Darcy listened as Tarah started hollering at Cooper. She put the phone down to inspect her face again, paying special attention to a tiny pimple just above her right eyebrow.

Why does it have to be there now, she thought, dabbing it with a bit of cover-up. She'd already covered it once, but she wanted to make sure it was invisible to Hakeem.

It wasn't the only thing she hoped to hide.

"Hello? You still there?" Tarah asked.

Darcy quickly grabbed the phone off the bathroom counter.

"Yeah, I'm leavin' right now," she

replied. A jolt of nervous energy raced down her back, making her stomach tremble. An hour of trying on different outfits, messing with her hair, and putting on makeup hadn't calmed her nerves. She still felt tense about seeing Hakeem again, especially after what happened over the summer.

"*You mean you didn't even leave yet?*" Tarah shouted. Darcy held the phone away from her ear again, but there was no escaping her friend's yelling. "We was supposed to meet fifteen minutes ago!"

"I know. I'm sorry, but things were busy at Scoops, and my manager made me stay late," Darcy lied, annoyed at herself for being dishonest with her best friend.

It was true the ice cream store had a busy day. Though it was early September, the weather was as hot as mid-July, and Scoops had been crammed with people buying ice cream. But Darcy's manager, Tamika Ardis, never asked her to stay late. Instead, she sent Darcy home early after she argued with a customer. Darcy had been rushing to prepare two milkshakes when she heard someone call out to her.

3

"Where's the rest of my change?"

Darcy turned to face a large woman with a tight weave. Two kids huddled close to the woman's legs, holding sticky, half-eaten ice cream cones that dripped onto the floor. Darcy had served them just a few minutes earlier.

"I already gave it to you, ma'am," Darcy replied.

"You better check your register or learn to count or somethin' 'cause I gave you a $20 bill. You just shortchanged me $10," the woman snapped, her free hand resting on her hips.

Darcy took a deep breath. All summer, she'd dealt with customers who treated her and her coworker Haley like trash. Usually Darcy just smiled and ignored it when people were mean, but today she didn't have any patience.

"You don't need to be rude, ma'am," Darcy replied. The words had slipped out so fast Darcy was stunned. So was Haley, who at that moment dropped a small chocolate sundae onto her cash register.

"*Excuse me*?" the woman said, nudging aside the person who'd been at the head of the line. "Girl, you best check that register and yo' mouth and give me

4

my change, or I'ma make a scene up in here."

"Ma'am, let me finish with this customer first, and I'll help you," Darcy replied, still holding the milkshakes in her hands.

"No, you're gonna help me *now*. I waited in line once. I ain't waitin' again."

Darcy felt her temper building. She couldn't tell the customer off; that would only get her fired. And she couldn't admit she was too stressed to focus on her work. That would only make the woman angrier. For several long seconds, Darcy didn't know what to say. Her mind had gone blank.

"It's okay, ma'am. I can help you," Tamika cut in just in time. "Let's check the register."

Darcy watched as her manager unlocked the cash drawer. She was sure she hadn't miscounted. In her months on the job, she had made plenty of mistakes, but never with money. At Scoops and at Bluford High where she was about to start her junior year, numbers were always something Darcy was good at.

But inside the cash drawer, Tamika found a $20 bill sitting in the $10 slot. Darcy knew instantly she had made a mistake, and the customer had been right. Darcy felt her cheeks burn with embarrassment.

"I'm so sorry, ma'am," Darcy said as Tamika handed over the money.

"Mmm hmm." The woman scowled and walked out with her children.

"What's wrong with you, Darcy? I've never seen you act that way, and I never want to see it again," Tamika warned as soon as the store emptied out. "I can't afford to upset customers. It's hard enough to stay in business around here as it is."

"I'm sorry. I just got a lot on my mind."

"I hope it's not serious, Darcy. I need you around here. I wish I had two of you."

"No, it's not. It's just . . ." Darcy paused, trying to decide how honest she should be. Tamika recently offered to increase her hours. Darcy didn't want her to change her mind.

"It's her boyfriend, I mean *ex-boyfriend*," cut in Haley, her blond pony-tail poking through the back of her green Scoops visor.

Darcy's jaw dropped. Haley had promised never to tell anyone what they discussed at work, especially not Tamika.

"He's been in Detroit for months, and tonight she's gonna see him for the first time since he got back. She doesn't want to admit it, but she's really excited," Haley continued with a smile. "And kinda nervous too."

"*Haley, shut your mouth!*" Darcy snapped, embarrassed to hear her personal life being discussed with her boss. "That was between you and me."

"Relax, Darcy. I'm just telling her why you're so out of it. It's not like she hasn't noticed. You're on another planet today," Haley explained.

"I'm *not* out of it. I just miscounted some change, that's all. Not like *you* never made a mistake, Haley."

"Don't even go there, Darce. This isn't about me, and you know it."

Darcy knew Haley was right. All day, she kept forgetting customers' orders. It got so bad she started writing everything down like her first week on the job. Even when she tried to listen to people, all Darcy could hear were the questions racing through her mind.

Should I tell Hakeem about what happened to me this summer?

If I tell him the truth, will he blame me

7

or think I'm a bad person?

Will we ever get back together?

"Haley's right," Tamika said, putting a hand on Darcy's shoulder.

"But—"

"It's okay, Darcy. I know you're a great worker, but today you're having a bad day. Lord knows I've had my share. When I think about it, almost all of them have to do with men," Tamika said with a knowing smile. "Why don't you take the rest of the afternoon off. Haley and I can handle things until closing."

"Are you serious?" Darcy asked. It felt wrong to have everyone know her business, but she needed the break to clear her head and get ready.

"Yeah, go and have fun. Not too much fun, though," Tamika said.

"And whatever you do, be sure someone else counts your change tonight," Haley teased.

Darcy left Scoops in a daze. It was true Hakeem distracted her from work, but there were other things tugging at her too. The summer had been like the earthquakes that sometimes cracked sidewalks and shattered windows in her neighborhood. Only this time, the quake centered on Darcy's house. She still felt aftershocks.

Grandma's quiet death in the bedroom next to Darcy's.

Her parents' announcement that they were having a baby.

Her old friend Brisana's pregnancy scare.

Deeper still was what happened one afternoon just after she and Hakeem broke up. That's when Brian Mason came around with his shiny red Toyota, his smooth voice and wide, dark shoulders. He was nineteen. Darcy babysat for his sister, Liselle. Just thinking of Brian made Darcy nauseous.

Should I tell Hakeem what happened?

For a while, it seemed like a question she wouldn't have to answer. The day Hakeem left, Darcy was sure she'd never see him again. His father was battling cancer, and his family was broke from medical bills. Their only choice was to move in with relatives in faraway Detroit. Hakeem and Darcy split up just before they left.

The loss crushed Darcy. Her boyfriend for most of their sophomore year, Hakeem had also been one of her closest friends at Bluford. He had stood by her no matter what drama was happening in her life, and there had been plenty, especially since her father returned after abandoning the family for five years. When they said goodbye for the last time, they promised to stay in touch and to always be honest with each other.

Darcy hadn't kept that promise.

For months, she ignored the voice in her head, the one that made her feel guilty whenever she stared at Hakeem's picture collecting dust in her room.

Then a miracle happened. Hakeem's father's health improved, and he allowed his son to live with Cooper and return to Bluford High. Darcy was thrilled beyond words at the news, but her past with Brian still haunted her.

There was no way she could tell Hakeem what happened. No way she could admit she'd gone to Brian's apartment to be alone with him. No way she could say Brian soothed the ache she felt when Hakeem left. And there was something else she couldn't confess to Hakeem.

Brian had gone too far. They had been on his couch kissing, and everything was okay until he tried to work his hands under her shirt.

"*Relax*," he said when she grabbed

his hand.

Then she felt him tugging at her clothes again. His scratchy palm slid against the sensitive skin of her stomach. This time, she told him point-blank to stop. She even tried to push him away. He got angry.

"You're acting like a baby!" he yelled. She tried to get off the couch, but he was too strong. Within seconds, he had her pinned. Sometimes she could still feel how he held her down, his hands gripping her like chains, his strong body pressing against hers. For a frightening instant, she realized she couldn't escape him.

But her father arrived and stopped Brian in his tracks.

"If you ever mess with my daughter again, it will be the last mistake you make!" Dad yelled with a wild rage in his eyes, slamming Brian against a wall. Brian moved out a few days later, but the damage was done.

For weeks afterward, Darcy relived the attacks in nightmares. In them, Brian was even more violent, and Dad never arrived to save her. The dreams got so severe she couldn't sleep. Then she started having panic attacks. Things got so bad Darcy told her parents and Tarah about her problem. She even met for weeks with a counselor at the community center where Tarah worked. Over time, the nightmares and panic attacks faded. But the scars were still there.

Darcy felt them gnawing at her as she left Scoops. Felt them as she prepared to meet Hakeem for the first time since he returned. Felt them even now as she spoke with Tarah on her cell phone.

"Look, Darce, are you comin' out or not?" Tarah asked, shattering her thoughts.

Darcy sighed and put her makeup away.

"I'll be there, Tar'," she said. "Ten minutes. I promise."

"If you're not, we're comin' over there and draggin' you out," Tarah warned.

"I'll be there," Darcy repeated, smoothing out her shirt one last time and inspecting the way her body filled her jeans. "I'm leaving right now."

Tarah hung up, and Darcy headed out the door, rushing toward Niko's.

Should I tell Hakeem what happened?

She still didn't know the answer.

Chapter 2

Darcy spotted everyone sitting at the usual table in the back corner of Niko's. The restaurant looked the same as always, crowded with Bluford students and other young people eating, talking, and laughing loudly.

But to Darcy, Niko's felt different since Hakeem left—smaller, though she knew it couldn't be.

"There she is!" shouted Cooper as soon as she neared the table. "Let's eat!"

"Coop, would you at least let her sit down first?" Tarah scolded.

"Sorry, y'all," Cooper said. "But I worked all day and didn't have no lunch break. If I don't get some pepperoni pizza right now, I'ma eat Darcy's chair. Then she won't have a place to sit."

"Coop!" Tarah yelled, slapping him

13

playfully in the chest.

"It's all right. I'm sorry I kept you all waiting. It's just been one of those days," Darcy said, glancing at Tarah and then Hakeem.

He stood up immediately in saggy jeans and a loose white T-shirt. Even in those clothes, Darcy could see he'd grown over the summer, not taller, but wider and more muscular. And he seemed older, too, and more handsome. For a split second, she could hear the voice in her head confessing everything to him.

While you were gone, I started seeing someone else. He tried to hurt me. It was a mistake. Please don't hate me. I still want us to get back together like old times.

But as she looked into his eyes, her mouth felt locked tight, as if an invisible hand gripped her face.

"Hi, Hakeem," she said, forcing herself to speak. She could barely manage a smile she was so tense.

Hakeem gave her a quick, firm hug, patting her back twice like she was his aunt. The touch made Darcy cringe inside. It was nothing like the embraces they'd shared only months ago.

"Good to s-s-see you, Darce," he said, looking at her quickly and turning away. Darcy was surprised to hear his stutter. It was a problem that surfaced when he was nervous or stressed. Normally it happened when he talked to adults, not with her.

"You too," she replied, wondering if her touch felt as uncomfortable as his.

Darcy felt Tarah watching them, trying to figure out what was wrong. Darcy wanted to talk to her alone but didn't know how to ask without seeming rude. Instead, she sat down at the table. Several seconds passed without a word. It felt like hours to Darcy.

"So can we eat?" Cooper blurted out, his voice shattering the heavy silence that gathered over their table like fog.

"Yeah, I been dreaming about Niko's pizza for months," Hakeem said, turning to Cooper and sitting down. "What are we waiting for?"

"Amen!" Coop shouted, jumping up to place the order.

For a second, the table got quiet again, and Darcy wondered what she could say that would seem natural. Looking at Hakeem, she could swear he felt just as awkward.

15

Was he holding something back too? She wondered.

"So can y'all believe it?" Tarah asked suddenly, her voice a bit forced. "We're juniors. I can't believe it myself. Where'd the time go?"

Hakeem sighed and rubbed his forehead.

Darcy squirmed in her seat, grateful to see Cooper return to the table. She knew Tarah was only trying to get them to talk, but her questions only made things more tense. Tarah's long stares didn't help either. Darcy felt like she was on one of those reality TV shows her younger sister Jamee watched where people pretended to act normal even though five cameras were in their faces.

"I hear what you sayin', girl," Cooper cut in. "Seems like yesterday Darcy was just a know-it-all in Ms. Reed's class who did nothin' but hit the books. Now we know she can hang, and we all tight."

"Thanks a lot, Coop," Darcy replied, remembering how at the beginning of last year, she and Tarah were nearly enemies. It was all ancient history.

"Seems like yesterday you had a big mouth and no sense. But nothin's changed, Coop, 'cause you actin' that

16

way right now," Tarah cut back, glaring at him.

"That's cold," he replied, acting hurt.

"But it's true," Tarah shot back.

"I know what Coop's trying to s-s-say," Hakeem spoke up suddenly. "Look how much we all changed in just one year. If Coop's mom didn't let me to stay at his crib, I wouldn't even be here. Who knows where we'll be a year from now."

"Man, Detroit sure made you serious, bro," Cooper said.

"It *is* serious, Coop. When my Dad got sick, I went from worrying about grades to wondering whether he'd even make it. I saw things change just like that," he snapped his fingers to make his point.

"Once you go through that, life ain't the same. You start thinking differently about everything. Maybe some things aren't what you thought they were. I don't mean to sound depressing, but the truth is you don't know what's gonna happen. We might not be here next week, forget about next year," Hakeem continued, looking at each person at the table as he spoke. There was a depth in his eyes that Darcy didn't remember. The summer had changed him too, no doubt about it.

"I know what you mean," Darcy replied. "I feel the same way. With Grandma passing away and the baby coming and . . ." she paused. She knew her thoughts were drifting toward Brian. She wasn't about to go there, not with everyone staring at her. Not with the strange, new Hakeem across from her. "You just change, you know. Some things don't seem as important as they used to."

Darcy felt a wave of sadness as she spoke. Maybe what they were really saying was that things were over between them. The months apart had destroyed what little remained of their friendship, dried it up like a plant left in the sun too long without water. Their old relationship was finally dead.

Tarah leaned forward, shaking her head as if what she heard bothered her.

"I hear what y'all are sayin', and I know you're bein' real, but you're forgettin' somethin'. Friends and family ain't like clothes that go out of style. You don't just drop your people." Tarah paused and looked at Darcy, then back to Hakeem. "When stuff happens, which it always does, you work through it.

That don't mean it's easy. I'd be lyin' if I said that. But it's what you gotta do when somethin's important."

Darcy shifted uncomfortably in her chair. She noticed Hakeem was playing with a straw, his eyes aimed down at the table, not at her.

"It's kinda like pizza," Cooper said.

Tarah rolled her eyes and shook her head in frustration.

"Yo, you *really* need to eat something, Coop," Hakeem added, smiling slightly.

"I'm serious. Check this out. Say you find something you really like—like pepperoni pizza. Why change anything if it's that good? If you did, you'd throw away something special. Once y'all try a slice, you'll see what I mean. Some things don't need to change." Cooper's eyes were fixed on Hakeem. Tarah's were too.

Hakeem grunted and tossed his straw aside. Darcy took a sip of water.

"Two pizzas?" the waiter interrupted, carrying two large trays.

"Yeah, you can put that one right in front of me," Cooper instructed.

Darcy smiled as Cooper quickly grabbed two slices, wincing as a glob of hot cheese landed on his wrist. Across from him, she noticed Hakeem's face. For several seconds, he didn't budge even though the pizza was right in front of him.

What's wrong with him? Darcy wondered. Though he was sitting next to her, Hakeem still seemed miles away.

Does he know I'm hiding something? Is that why he's so different? Or is it something else?

"You all right, Darce?" Tarah asked.

"Huh?" Darcy said. She noticed Cooper and Hakeem weren't at the table. They were standing in line at the cash register.

"What's botherin' you, girl? You hardly said anything tonight, and you only ate one slice of pizza. You feelin' okay?"

Darcy realized she'd been so distracted she didn't even see Cooper and Hakeem get up. She must have zoned out for at least a few minutes. "I'm fine, Tarah. I just got a lot on my mind, that's all," Darcy explained.

In line at the register, Cooper and Hakeem spoke quietly to each other. Darcy noticed Cooper did most of the talking.

"Well, spit it out, girl. You look more like you just said goodbye to Hakeem, not hello," Tarah said.

"I know, Tar. I'm sorry, it's just . . . " Darcy paused, lowering her voice so no one but Tarah could hear. "It's me and Hakeem. You saw how weird we were tonight. I never thought I'd say it, but I think it's finally over," she admitted. There was something sad and final in the word *over*. It seemed to echo in the air as she said it.

"C'mon, Darce! Hakeem just got back. Give him some time, girl. You both just need to get used to each other again. And you two need to talk and deal with what happened this summer so you can move on, you know. Just don't worry," Tarah said, rubbing her back.

Darcy wanted the words to be true, but she didn't believe them, not with what she'd just heard.

"You know what else?" she added, lowering her voice further so it was barely louder than a whisper. "I keep thinking about what happened with Brian. How am I ever gonna tell Hakeem about that? He'd never understand. He'd hate me."

Tarah sighed and rubbed Darcy's back without saying a word. Usually, she had a quick answer for everything. The fact that Tarah took so long to respond made Darcy feel even worse. It was like having a disease the doctor could not cure. Tarah might as well have come out and said, *"Yep, you're right, girl. You screwed up big-time, and ain't nothin' gonna fix it. Sorry."*

"Give it time, girl," Tarah said finally. "When you're ready, tell him what you need to tell him. If he's the person I think he is, he'll handle it just right. If not, you're better off without him." She stopped to eat a piece of hardened cheese she'd picked off the tray in front of her. "Like I said, both of you need to talk and sort things out. You don't need to rush anything. But I'm bein' straight up with you about this. I think you two can work everything out."

"Are you serious, Tarah? You really think so? You're not just saying that?" Darcy stared into Tarah's eyes, searching for a reason to believe her.

While Tarah didn't look away, she paused just a bit. Maybe no one else would have noticed it, but Darcy did.

"You know it, girl."

The two were quiet for a minute as Darcy replayed Tarah's words over and over again in her mind. The way she'd paused didn't sound right. Like an off-key voice in a choir. And there was something strange in Tarah's advice too.

"*You two need to deal with what happened this summer*," she had said. "*Both of you need to sort things out.*" Those words: *you two. Both of you.* What did they mean? Did Tarah know more than she was saying?

Darcy was about to ask when Hakeem and Cooper returned.

"Well, we should get back. First day of school is tomorrow," Hakeem said. "I still got some unpacking to do."

First day of school. The words seemed like a cruel joke, but they were true. Tomorrow would pile classes and homework on top of everything else swirling in Darcy's head. But no matter what her classes would bring, Darcy knew one question she needed an answer to first.

What happened to Hakeem this summer?

Chapter 3

Darcy rushed home to call Tarah. She'd just crossed the street onto her block when she heard people arguing. The street was mostly empty, so Darcy figured one of her elderly neighbors was watching TV with the volume turned way up. But as she got closer to her doorstep, Darcy realized the sound was coming from inside her house.

"Forget about it, Mattie!" Dad yelled as Darcy open the door. His voice boomed from the kitchen. "You are *not* going to do that. I won't allow it. End of story."

Darcy was shocked. Dad had never spoken to her mother that way. She rushed in to see what was happening.

"You don't get to tell me what I can and can't do, Carl!" Mom hollered back. She was standing in the middle of the

24

kitchen, her arms crossed over her chest. She was still wearing the ID badge from the hospital where she worked as an emergency room nurse. Dad was at the sink washing dishes. Both of them looked exhausted and upset. Neither seemed to notice Darcy standing in the hallway.

"I do when it comes to the health of my child," Dad replied. "Stop being so stubborn, Mattie!"

"Don't talk to me in that tone of voice. You got no right." Mom fumed, her jaw jutting out sharply with anger.

Darcy froze, afraid to get between them while they were fighting. Just then, Jamee came out of her bedroom and joined her in the hallway. Jamee gaped as if she couldn't believe what she was seeing.

"I'm that baby's father, Mattie. That's all the right I need," Dad challenged.

For weeks, Darcy had sensed the tension building in the house. The clues were everywhere, in the way her mother sighed whenever anyone talked about money, in the desperate way her father searched the newspaper for job listings, in the long walks he took alone in the evenings.

It started when his hours were cut at the fancy clothing store where he worked as a salesperson. Since then, her mother and father were always tense. Mom walked around with dark, baggy circles under her eyes. Dad talked less and seemed moody, always shuffling papers and rushing off to go somewhere. About the only thing that seemed to cheer them up was when they talked about the baby, but even the joy of that news had faded recently.

Sometimes, late at night, Darcy would listen to them exchanging words with each other. She knew they'd been trying to hide their problems from her and Jamee, but it wasn't working. Darcy figured a major fight was coming, but she never imagined it would be this loud and hurtful, or that it would explode like a bomb the night before the first day of school.

"You lost *that* right when you walked out on us, Carl! You haven't earned it back yet," Mom lashed back. "I worked fifty to sixty hours a week for the first few years after you left us for that other woman. I can do it again if I have to."

Dad tipped forward as if he'd been kicked in the stomach.

Crash!

The large plate in his hand fell to the kitchen floor and shattered.

Darcy's jaw dropped. She looked at Jamee, who had tears in her eyes. She grabbed her hand and fought the urge to jump in between her parents. It was like watching a horrible accident happen right in front of her eyes.

Dad slammed his fists on the counter and stepped away from the sink, crunching pieces of the broken plate under his feet. His face was twisted with pain, an image out of a nightmare.

Darcy knew mom's words hurt. Dad's biggest regret was that he'd started drinking and walked out on his family, leaving them for five long years. Since he'd returned last fall, he'd done nothing but apologize and try to undo the damage he caused.

"Why do you *always* have to go there, Mattie?" her father asked. His normally strong voice shook with emotion, a terrible sad sound that made Darcy want to cover her ears. "That was years ago, and it has nothing to do with us right now. We're both different people. I apologized a thousand times, but you just won't let it go."

27

"Because whenever I start to depend on you, I remember what happened the last time I did. I'm sorry, but this ain't easy for me, Carl. And your plan—to be a nighttime cab driver—is not gonna solve our problems."

"It's only until I find something better, Mattie," Dad explained. "Besides, I know this city well enough to stay out of the bad areas. And I can handle myself. Remember, I did some boxing in the Army."

"No, it's still not safe, Carl," Mom insisted. "I've seen too many cabbies in the ER. With a baby on the way, you've got to think about the bigger picture. We can't afford to have something happen to you."

"Mattie, I *am* thinking about the bigger picture. I'm a black man in this city in my forties without a college degree. Right now, I've gotta take whatever I can get. When I find something better, I'll move on. But I'm not gonna sit still and let you work sixty hours a week, especially when you're carrying our baby. Don't ask me to let that happen, 'cause I can't do it."

Dad stared at her as he spoke. Mom grabbed a broom and dustpan from the tiny kitchen closet. Darcy admired what her father was saying. She knew mom shouldn't work any more hours in the hospital than she had to. Even before she was pregnant, she would come home tired. But lately she seemed more weary than ever. Dad was just trying to help out. He was taking the job for the family, not himself.

"Well you should have thought about that before," Mom snapped. "I told you I wasn't ready to do this again, and you said not to worry. And now look at us. We got all these new bills for this house *you* wanted. We got a child on the way, and the only job you can find is one that has you drivin' in the 'hood at two in the morning! Now you see why I'm upset. You asked me to trust you, and look what *you* did. You got us into trouble again, Carl. I shoulda known better than to listen to you!"

"That's not fair, Mattie."

"You want to know what's not fair, Carl? That I dealt with your mistakes alone for five long years, and now you're asking me to do it again," she yelled, her words like sharp knives.

Dad shook his head. "I don't know why I even bother tryin' to talk to you

29

sometimes," he said, drying his hands on his pants. He stepped over the mess on the kitchen floor and practically ran into Darcy and Jamee. He stared at them, sighed, and then grabbed his keys.

"Where are you going?" Mom asked as he put on his old baseball cap and jacket.

Without a word, Dad walked out, slamming the door behind him.

Mom raced past Darcy and Jamee to the doorway.

"So that's it? You just gonna walk out again? You haven't changed one bit, Carl!" Mom yelled so loud the whole block could hear her voice. "*Not one bit!*"

Darcy wanted to follow him—anything to get away from the house, which suddenly felt more like a prison than a home.

"What are you two looking at?" Mom said, turning to them like the argument was their fault. Darcy knew it wasn't the time to talk to her mother, not with the veins in her forehead bulging with anger, not with the tears in her eyes.

"C'mon, Jamee," Darcy said, tugging her sister by her sleeve.

"No, Darcy," Jamee refused, shrugging Darcy off and turning to mom. "I'm not going anywhere. You're not fair, Mom. He's only tryin' to help. You can't work those hours anymore. It's not good for the baby. And if you keep treatin' Dad like that, he's gonna run away again."

"*Jamee!*" Darcy yelled. She couldn't believe her ears. Nothing had hurt Mom more than when Dad left with another woman. Sometimes Darcy still had flashbacks to her mother crying like a baby in Grandma's arms. It was the saddest sound she'd ever heard. Now Jamee was practically blaming mom for what happened. It was the most hurtful thing she could have said.

In one swift move, Mom stepped forward and swung her arm with her hand outstretched.

Slap!

Mom's palm struck Jamee's cheek, knocking her back into a wall. Darcy winced at the cracking sound, which seemed to boom through the air like a gunshot.

Her mother hadn't hit either of them in years. But the look in her angry, unblinking eyes said she might do it again.

Jamee's mouth was wide open with shock. She rubbed her face where

31

Mom's hand struck her. Darcy moved in between them. She had to do something to stop things from getting worse.

"Don't, Mom! Jamee didn't mean it that way," Darcy said as Mom moved closer.

"Don't you *ever* talk to me like that again! You hear me!" Mom screamed, pointing at Jamee. Darcy stood between them bracing herself.

"Mom, please—"

"And you stay out of this too, Darcy. This is between your father and me."

"What's your problem? We're in this family too," Jamee yelled, still rubbing her cheek. Darcy could hear the hurt and outrage in her voice.

"Jamee, just shut up!" Darcy said, grabbing Jamee's shoulders to calm her.

"Don't touch me!" Jamee yelled, shoving her hands aside.

Mom stormed down the hallway into her bedroom. She slammed the door behind her, knocking an old picture of Grandma to the floor. Jamee rushed the opposite way, out the front door.

Darcy stood in the suddenly quiet hallway alone.

It was as if a bomb had exploded, splitting the house into hundreds of pieces, leaving everyone too wounded to speak.

Darcy went out looking for Jamee ten minutes later.

She found her sitting on the front step of their house. It was dark, but Jamee's face was lit by the glow of a cigarette that dangled from her mouth. Supposedly she'd given up smoking last year after she dumped her abusive boyfriend, Bobby Wallace.

"Leave me alone," Jamee said coldly. "And don't lecture me about smoking. I know it's no good for me. Right now, I really don't care."

Darcy sat down next to her without a word. Her foot knocked over a beer bottle left on the sidewalk in front of their house. It rolled loudly into the dark. Even in the shadows, Darcy could see Jamee's eyes were swollen, her face wet with tears.

"Would you just go back inside," Jamee growled. "I don't need you out here. I don't need anybody."

Darcy put her hand on her sister's back. At first Jamee squirmed away, but then she stopped moving and let Darcy's arm rest on her shoulder.

"What's happening to us, Darce?" Jamee asked.

"It's just a fight, that's all. You always accuse me of worrying too much. Look at you now," Darcy said, wishing her words were more helpful, more convincing. But after the day she had, it was all she could think of. "They'll be okay. We'll be okay. I promise."

Jamee sniffled and wiped her eyes. "I miss Grandma," she said.

"Me too, Jamee," Darcy said, feeling the words deep in her chest. Grandma had always been the refuge they could go to, no matter what happened. Her absence left a gaping hole in Darcy's heart, one that seemed wider than ever. "Me too."

Jamee quietly took the cigarette from her mouth and crushed it into the ground. For several minutes, they didn't say anything.

"What if he leaves us again?" she asked.

It was a question Darcy asked herself many times since Dad had returned. For a while, she hadn't allowed herself to believe he was back. That way she could never be hurt again. But after all the helpful things he did over the past year, she gradually began to believe in him. And with the house, the new baby, and Grandma gone, she could not imagine him ever leaving.

But what happened tonight never happened before. A line had been crossed. What once seemed rock solid now felt like it had deep cracks. Like it could all come crashing down one day soon, a landslide that would claim her family as its victims.

"He won't," Darcy said, trying to convince herself as much as her sister. "He wouldn't do that again."

It was well past midnight when Darcy finally crawled into bed to sleep. In the kitchen, the shattered plate still littered the floor.

And her father hadn't come home.

Chapter 4

Darcy woke up with the worst headache.

It was 6:45 when she slammed the snooze button of her blaring alarm clock, hoping last night's fight was just another bad dream and summer break wasn't over.

But when she crawled out of bed, Darcy discovered her mother in the kitchen sweeping pieces of the broken plate into a dustpan. It was all too real.

"Dad's not back yet?" she asked.

"*No*," Mom said sternly, dumping the dustpan into the trash. She looked like she hadn't slept at all. Darcy could tell from her puffy, swollen eyes that she'd been crying.

"Where is he?"

"How should I know?" Mom snapped.

"No phone call. No nothing. I don't know what that man's doing."

Darcy cringed inside. She knew what those words sounded like, how they opened up old wounds. She was sure Dad was coming back, that he'd just gotten really upset from her mother's harsh words. What Mom said wasn't fair, but that didn't give Dad the right to just walk out without a word. Not with the painful memories of the past still haunting them all, especially not with Mom being pregnant.

"I'm sure he's comin' back—"

"I don't want to hear it. I am so mad at him right now, I can't even think straight," her mother warned.

Darcy wished she could do something to calm her. Anything. "Mom, I saved some money working at Scoops. If you need it, you and Dad can have it. And I can work more hours if it helps. Tamika even asked if I—"

"No," Mom said. "That's *your* money. I won't have you payin' for our mess. If I gotta work overtime to keep a roof over our head, that's what I'll do."

"But what about the baby, Mom? You can't do what you used—"

"Now don't *you* start with me. I can

37

and I will," Mom said. Her words were firm, but there was something hollow in the way she said them. Darcy also noticed she swept the floor too forcefully, spreading the shards of the broken plate instead of sweeping them up.

"Here, let me help you, Mom," Darcy said, reaching for the broom.

"The best way you can help me right now is to leave me alone," her mother grumbled.

"But Mom—"

"Just go, Darcy. Get ready for school," Mom insisted. "I'll take care of this."

Darcy forced herself out of the kitchen, pretending not to see the tears in her mother's tired eyes.

Darcy heard the front door open just as she finished getting dressed. She was sure Dad had finally come home, but when she walked into the living room, she didn't find her father. Instead, she saw Jamee rushing down the street. Darcy shook her head in frustration. Jamee had left for school without her.

Outside, the sun hung bright and golden over the neighborhood, making Darcy squint as she walked out the door. Though it was early, she could already feel the heat building and knew it was going to be another summery day. But the sunlight only mocked her gloomy mood.

Clusters of students headed quietly down the street toward Bluford High School. Many of them looked young and scared as they slowly passed Niko's, the Golden Grill Restaurant, and the Korean grocery store.

"Have a good day, Harold," said an old woman from the third floor window of a nearby apartment building. She had a friendly, round face, and she waved gently to a thick-bodied boy standing on the sidewalk in front of Darcy.

"Thanks, Grandma," he replied somberly. He spoke like he was heading to a funeral, not his first day of high school. He looked a bit embarrassed when he saw Darcy pass by.

Darcy smiled, remembering how nervous she'd been on her first day at Bluford. She was so scared she almost got sick to her stomach. Mom had to work that day, and Dad was long gone, so Grandma decided to walk her to the front door of the school to make her feel better.

"Don't you worry, Angelcake. You're gonna shine at this school. I know it. One day, you'll look back at this moment, smile, and wonder where all the time went. You mark my words."

Two years had passed since that day, and already Darcy knew Grandma was right. If only she could still talk to her. Tell her about the new baby, about the troubles at home with Dad. Get her advice about Hakeem.

Hakeem. In all the drama at home, Darcy had almost forgotten about the awkward dinner at Niko's. She had to talk to Tarah right away and find out what was wrong with him.

Up ahead on the other side of the street, Darcy spotted a couple her age holding hands and laughing. She couldn't help but stare at them as they strolled together in the morning sun. Seeing them made Darcy feel even more miserable.

See what you lost, they seemed to say.

Darcy walked faster just so she wouldn't have to look at them. After a few minutes, she reached the supermarket parking lot that bordered Bluford and glimpsed the main steps leading to the

40

school's front doors. Three security guards in blue uniforms stood with Ms. Spencer, the school principal, at the top of the steps. They were checking students with metal detectors as they entered. Next to the school, Darcy could see the blue and yellow sign hanging behind the bleachers of the football field.

Welcome to Bluford High School
Home of the Buccaneers

Even though she'd been there two years, Darcy still felt her stomach jump at the sight of the school. Taking a deep breath, she climbed the main steps to begin her junior year.

The hallway inside was crowded with students rushing in all directions. Many of them were holding schedules and looking at room numbers trying to figure out where they were going.

Freshmen, Darcy thought to herself.

Ahead of her, Darcy spotted Jamee standing with Amberlynn Bailey and Cindy Gibson. The two girls had been her sister's closest friends since elementary school. Each had an arm around Jamee, who wiped her eyes several times.

Though she couldn't hear them,

Darcy knew exactly what they were talking about: last night. She passed them, glad to see Jamee had friends to support her, though she suddenly felt alone in the crowded hallway. She wondered where Tarah, Hakeem, and Cooper were.

"There you are! Oh my God, Darcy. We need to talk," said a voice, snapping Darcy from her thoughts.

Darcy turned to see Brisana Meeks. Before last year, Brisana had been her best friend. But everything changed when Darcy started hanging out with Tarah and Cooper, people Brisana hated. Since then, the two had good days and bad days. Darcy hoped this would be a good one.

"What's up, Bris?" Darcy asked, doing her best to smile. She noticed Brisana looked better than ever. She was wearing a sleeveless gray shirt that hugged her body and revealed her curvy figure. Her hair was long and braided with copper highlights, and her cocoa skin was flawless.

What a change from July, Darcy thought, remembering Brisana sobbing in the tiny parking lot behind Scoops. Back then, Brisana thought she was pregnant, and she came to Darcy for help.

42

Darcy was stunned at the news. For years, Brisana, a fellow honors student, had looked down on people who struggled in school, especially girls who got pregnant.

"That's just dumb. Why would you let something like that happen?" she'd once said about Liselle Mason, a girl they knew who quit school to have a baby.

But then Brisana fell for an older guy who told her he loved her. Darcy knew he was no good. She'd seen him flirting with other girls, but Brisana was blind. Soon she was in over her head, making the same mistakes Liselle made. And because she'd been such a snob, Brisana had few friends to turn to. That's why she came to Darcy. Brisana practically admitted it the morning they went to the clinic and learned the pregnancy scare was a false alarm.

Darcy hoped the episode would change Brisana, make her less likely to judge others. Maybe even help her become friends with Tarah, a girl who was her opposite in many ways. But looking at her now, Darcy saw nothing to indicate she'd changed. If anything, Brisana looked even more her old self, like she was a song on the radio and someone just turned it louder.

"Look, Darcy, I have something to tell you that you're not gonna want to hear," Brisana said. She had the I-have-a-secret look in her eyes. Darcy had seen it a thousand times before, especially when Brisana was about to gossip. "It's about Hakeem," she added.

"What about him?"

"He's back."

"I know, Brisana. I went out with him last night," Darcy said, sighing with relief. "Why would that be bad news?"

"Listen, Darce. I saw him at the mall Saturday. He was with another girl." She looked into Darcy's eyes as she spoke as if she was trying to see the impact of her words.

Alarms began sounding in Darcy's head. The last time Brisana had given her advice about Hakeem, it was a lie. Brisana had always been jealous of her relationship with Hakeem. Last year she'd even tried to break them up by saying false things about him. But that was so long ago, Darcy was shocked to hear her trying it again.

"C'mon, Bris. I thought we were done all this," she said.

"I'm serious," Brisana insisted. "I

44

watched them in the food court, Darcy. And from what I could see, they weren't there to eat."

Brisana's story made no sense. Hakeem had barely been back three days. How could he have another girl-friend already? And why was Brisana, the person furthest from Hakeem, the only one who knew about it? There was only one reason: the story was another lie. Brisana wanted to stop them from getting back together. Darcy was sure of it.

"I'm not hearing this," Darcy said, turning and walking down the hallway. Brisana raced to keep up.

"Darcy, I saw him with my own two eyes. I swear."

Darcy wished Brisana's voice sound-ed less honest. Wished that her stare seemed less sincere.

"Whatever."

"Darcy, I don't know who this girl is. But she looks like she stepped out of a magazine or something. She is *all that*," Brisana said.

"Just stop it, okay! I don't want to hear it," Darcy replied, walking faster. "I really thought we were cool. Since you're lying to me again, I guess I was wrong," Darcy said, acting as if Brisana's words didn't shake her.

"*Lying* to you! Is that what you think I'm doing?" Brisana fumed. "Fine. Be that way. But don't say I didn't tell you. And don't come crying later on just 'cause you were too stubborn to listen."

"If I remember correctly, *you* were the one who came crying to me this summer, so don't try acting like you're all special," Darcy yelled. She knew her words were mean, but at that moment she didn't care.

Brisana gasped as if she'd just been slapped, but Darcy ignored her.

Darcy stormed through the hallway, forcing several freshmen to step aside as she rushed to the closest restroom. Inside, the air was a thick mixture of cleanser, perfume, and a touch of cigarette smoke. Girls hurried in and out, washing their hands, fixing their make-up, inspecting their clothes and hair.

"Oh my God! Tyray looks so *good*," said one girl.

"He does," replied another. "I bet he's a player, though."

Darcy wanted to scream.

She went into a stall, locked it shut, and put her hands over her ears to block out the sounds around her.

But inside her head, voices of doubt were speaking.

And with each second, they grew a bit louder.

Chapter 5

Looks like she stepped out of a magazine . . .
More than friends . . .
Don't say I didn't tell you . . .

Brisana's words echoed in Darcy's mind as she made her way to Ms. York's algebra II class. Even as she sat down at a desk in the center of the classroom, Darcy could barely hear what the teacher was saying over the sound of Brisana's voice in her head. She was remembering Hakeem's strange behavior at Niko's when she felt someone tap her shoulder.

"Yo, pay attention. She's calling you," a voice said.

Darcy turned around to see Roylin Bailey sitting at the desk behind her. He nodded toward the front of the room.

"Huh?" Darcy asked in confusion. She glanced forward and noticed the whole class staring at her. Ms. York, the pear-shaped woman sitting at the teacher's desk, raised her eyebrows. She held a red pen in her hand, and a black notebook was open in front of her.

"I think you should mark Darcy absent, Ms. York. She's somewhere else right now," Roylin teased. Several people in class laughed.

"Perhaps Mr. Bailey has a point," the teacher said, giving Darcy a stern look.

Darcy immediately realized what happened. She had zoned out again, this time during attendance. She could feel her face burning with embarrassment.

"I'm here . . . sort of," Darcy said, trying to make a joke out of what happened. "Sorry."

"We're glad you're with us, Ms. Wills," Ms. York said, marking her notebook and moving on to the next person.

For the rest of class, Darcy tried to focus on Ms. York's quick review of concepts from geometry and algebra I. But her mind kept wandering to Brisana's warning and the odd way Hakeem acted the night before. The more she thought about it, the more Darcy wondered if there might be some truth to what Brisana told her.

Tarah would know. She would ask her during lunch period.

Or just talk to him, Darcy thought to herself. But doing so meant she would have to be honest about Brian. She'd have to admit what happened and what almost happened.

"Is everything okay, Ms. Wills?" a voice suddenly disrupted her thoughts.

"Huh?"

"Class is over. Unless you wish to sit with the freshman I have next period, I suggest you go to your next class."

"Yes, ma'am," Darcy said, realizing she had done it again. "I just have a lot on my mind," she added, closing her notebook and heading toward the door.

"I can see that," the teacher nodded. "But tomorrow I expect you to actually attend my class, Ms. Wills. Understand?"

"Yes, Ms. York."

Darcy felt the sweat beading on her forehead as she bolted out of the classroom. She had to find out the truth about Hakeem soon.

Before it got her fired from Scoops and flunked out of Bluford.

"Oh my God! You in here too? That's what I'm talkin' 'bout," Tarah cheered and strutted through the doorway of Darcy's third class, chemistry.

Darcy had arrived early and sat in the front row, determined to pay attention. She had no idea Tarah was in the class, but as soon as she saw her, she was relieved. Now she could finally get some answers.

"We gonna have some fun in here, girl. Just like old times back in Ms. Reed's class. You gotsta be my lab partner again," Tarah added, dropping her shiny neon pink backpack down with a loud thud.

Darcy noticed Tarah got her nails done for the first day of school. Each finger ended in a long fake nail coated in colorful designs that sparkled with glittery polish.

"My cousin's friend hooked me up last night after we got back. Ain't they da bomb?" Tarah said, spreading her thick fingers so Darcy could inspect them.

To Darcy, the nails looked like painted claws, not something she would ever wear. Especially not for the lab assignments they might do in chemistry class, but she wasn't about to say anything. Her mind was on Hakeem.

"They're really nice, Tar," she said quickly, trying her best to sound sincere, though she knew Tarah was too smart to be fooled. "Listen, I need to talk to you about something serious."

"What is it, Darce? Everything okay at home?" Tarah asked, reaching to get something from her backpack.

Darcy paused for a minute. She wasn't ready to go near what happened at home. It was all too much, and Brisana's words were still fresh in her mind. She needed answers about Hakeem. *Now.*

"Go on, girl. Spit it out."

"It's Hakeem. I think he's hiding something from me."

"*Hiding something?*" Tarah repeated, her voice a bit louder than usual.

"Think about it, Tar. The summer's a long time. What if he started seeing someone in Detroit?" Darcy said, watching Tarah's face for clues.

"C'mon, Darce. Why you gotta go there?" Tarah asked as if the idea was crazy. But there was a sad note in her voice, and she avoided looking directly into Darcy's eyes.

Just then, Brisana Meeks walked

into the classroom.

Darcy remained still as Brisana strolled by and grabbed a desk two rows away without even looking in their direction. She knew Brisana had seen her talking to Tarah. Brisana could size up a room better than anyone.

"You would tell me if you knew something, right?" Darcy asked, keeping her voice low.

For a second, Tarah looked like she was in pain. She took a deep breath, glanced quickly at Brisana and then focused on Darcy. "Look, it's like I told you last night. You two need to talk. When you do, things'll be all right. And no matter what happens, y'all will still be friends, right?"

Darcy nearly fell out of her seat.

Friends. It was the "f" word that meant she and Hakeem were completely over. Tarah had never said it before about the two of them. She might as well have just said, *"Give it up, girl. It's over."*

"So it's true then?" Darcy asked, unable to keep her voice down. She could feel eyes watching her, but she didn't care. "He's seeing someone? Come on, Tarah. What's going on?"

Tarah sighed, put both her hands

up, and turned her head away from Darcy. "Look, I'm sorry, girl, but I don't want to be in the middle of a fight between you two. Like I said last night, you just need to talk to Hakeem. He's the one you need to speak to about this, not me."

"*What?*" Darcy gasped. That Tarah said the word *fight* was all the proof she needed. "So all this time you knew something was going on and you hid it from me?"

"I knew this was gonna happen," Tarah said, slumping back in her chair. "Look, I'm sorry, Darcy. I mean it. But from now on, I'm not gonna say nothin' till you talk to Hakeem. I'm outta this."

Darcy couldn't believe her ears. Tarah had practically been lying right to her face. And how long had it been going on? Two days? Two months? Darcy's mind began spinning. She felt like she'd just been kicked in the stomach and slapped in the face at the same time.

"I can't believe you. I trusted you with everything, Tarah. How could you do this? You're supposed to be my friend!" Darcy exclaimed.

"I *am* your friend. But I'm Hakeem's friend too," Tarah replied. "I've known

54

him since we was five-years-old. Him and Coop's like brothers, and I hear everything because of that. But it ain't right for me to be tellin' everybody's secrets, especially when the secrets can hurt people."

"That's not right, Tarah. After everything I've told you, you shouldn't be lying to me about Hakeem—"

"Don't get in my face callin' me a liar. Nothin' I said was a lie, and I gave you both the same advice: Talk to each other. Maybe I kept Hakeem's secret. But I also kept yours," Tarah said, sitting up and waving her long-nailed finger at Darcy. "Remember, you haven't told *him* everything either."

Darcy felt her pulse throb and her ears begin to ring. For a second, she wanted to slap Tarah's wide face. Who was she to practically bring up Brian in the middle of a crowded classroom? How dare she act like Darcy's secret was the same as hiding the truth about Hakeem?

"I can't believe you just said that! That's totally different—"

"Why?" Tarah challenged. "You two are supposed to be close, but you keep stuff from him. He keeps it from you. What's different about that?"

55

"But I trusted you—"

"I didn't break no promises to you," Tarah cut back. "I ain't done nothin' but try to get you two to talk since he got back. Only difference is you want me to tell you his secrets and hide yours. That ain't right. And it ain't fair to expect me to do that."

"*Fair?*" Darcy yelled back. She couldn't believe how angry she was at Tarah. Since they became friends, she never imagined a time they could yell at each other. But now she couldn't stop.

"I'll tell you what fair is, Tarah. Fair is being straight up with me. Fair is telling me the truth when you say nothing's wrong. Fair is knowing that what happened to me this summer is different than Hakeem kissing some girl at the mall on Saturday. If I saw Cooper doing that, you'd be the first person I'd tell no matter what he said 'cause it's the right thing to do," Darcy hammered back.

"I been tryin' to do the right thing, Darcy. But I couldn't tell you 'cause if I did, you'd lose it, and there'd be no chance of you and Hakeem getting back together," Tarah admitted.

"Well, there's no chance of that now," Darcy said. "We're done."

"Aww snap!" said a boy at the front of the classroom.

Tarah shook her head in frustration. Darcy knew Brisana was taking in every word, but she didn't care.

Just then, someone snickered, and Darcy noticed that everyone in the class had suddenly turned toward the front of the room. She looked up and saw a middle-aged white man in tan pants and a lab coat. He was sitting on top of the teacher's desk. Darcy had not even heard him enter the classroom.

"Are you two finished?" he asked. Someone giggled.

Overhead the bell signaling the start of class blared loudly, breaking the moment.

Darcy took a deep breath. She swallowed down her anger like a poison that left a bitter taste in her mouth.

"Yeah, we're done all right," she grumbled.

"Aww, c'mon, Darce," Tarah whispered, crossing her arms and slumping back in her chair. "Don't be that way."

Darcy could feel tears trying to gather in her eyes. But her resentment was stronger, holding the tears back, planting the hurt deep in her gut where it could grow like a tumor.

As soon as class ended, Darcy stood up at her desk. She saw Tarah attempt to reach out to her and heard the beginning of an apology.

But it didn't matter.

Without a word, Darcy turned around, grabbed her things, and walked out, leaving her old friend behind.

Chapter 6

At lunchtime, Darcy looked for Hakeem but couldn't find him. She didn't know his schedule and wasn't about to ask Tarah for it. All she could do was wait until the end of the day. Then she'd tell him what was on her mind and end it once and for all.

In the cafeteria, she grabbed a soda and headed to an empty table. She wanted to be as far from Tarah as possible. Just thinking about how Tarah had hidden the truth from her made Darcy's stomach turn.

So what if Hakeem was her friend too.

So what if she knew Hakeem longer.

So what if she tried to get us to talk.

Tarah still should have told me everything, Darcy thought as she sipped her soda and flipped through the few notes she managed to take in chemistry class.

"I told you, Darcy," said a voice, interrupting her. She looked up to see Brisana carrying a lunch tray. A thin smile stretched across her face.

"Don't start with me right now, Brisana," Darcy grumbled, closing her notebook. "I know you just want to rub it in."

"That's not true. Believe me, if I wanted to do that, you'd know it," Brisana said, sitting down across from her. "I just wanted to see how you're doing, that's all."

"How do you think I'm doing?" Darcy muttered. "My boyfriend, I mean *ex*-boyfriend, found someone else, and my best friend lied to hide it from me."

"You mean *ex*-best friend," Brisana said, eyeing Darcy carefully.

"Yeah, I guess so," Darcy replied with a shrug, her anger pushing the sadness away, but just barely.

"I don't mean to be rude, but what did you think was gonna happen?" Brisana said, sprinkling dressing on a small salad she got for lunch. "I mean, Hakeem's a guy. You two broke up. Did you think he was gonna stay single forever?"

"No, but—"

"And Tarah's always been closer to Cooper and Hakeem than to you. Now that Hakeem's living with her boyfriend, it's only gonna get worse."

"Yeah, but—"

"I mean I bet they all decided months ago to lie to you, the way *they* talk," Brisana said, rolling her eyes.

Darcy's blood was boiling. She hated to think of them all getting together and deciding to keep the secret from her, but it made sense.

That would explain the silences at Niko's. The strange glances. Darcy felt like her head was about to explode, like she was the plate Dad shattered into a thousand useless pieces.

"If you ask me," Brisana continued, slicing through a piece of lettuce, "I think you need to get real, Darcy. Those people are never gonna change. You need to move on. Not just from Hakeem, but from all of them."

Darcy tossed her notebook into her book bag. She didn't want to admit it, but for once she agreed with Brisana's advice. If Tarah, Cooper, and Hakeem had no trouble lying to her, what kind of friends were they? She imagined what

61

they must have said to each other before they went to Niko's.

"Don't worry, bro. I ain't gonna say nothin' to her," Cooper probably said. Darcy could almost see him slapping hands with Hakeem.

"She won't hear nothin' from me neither," Tarah would have replied.

Thinking about it made Darcy want to scream. And deep down beneath the white hot anger that stormed in her chest, Darcy felt something else even stronger than rage. She felt pain.

It hurt that Hakeem had already replaced her. It hurt that their friends had helped hide his secret. Hurt that the trust she had put in them was broken, that the friendship she depended on each day was not what she thought it was.

You need to move on. Brisana's advice made sense.

"Maybe you're right," Darcy said, though she wished it weren't true. "I guess I was wrong about all of them."

"It's okay, Darce," Brisana replied with a grin that was somehow both warm and cold at the same time. *"I'm* still your friend."

Darcy's hands were shaking when

the final bell rang.

She rushed to her locker, grabbed her books and headed out the front doors of Bluford ready to confront Hakeem.

At the bottom of the steps, she joined a few other students leaning against a fence watching people exit the building. As Darcy waited, her heart racing, hundreds of kids slowly poured out of the school. Some got into cars, others hopped onto yellow buses lined outside, and many just walked home.

The first person Darcy recognized was her sister. Darcy hoped Jamee wouldn't see her, but their eyes met. Jamee headed straight to her with a wide smile on her face.

"Oh my God, Darce! I had the best day," Jamee gushed. "Me, Amberlynn, and Cindy are in the same English class with your old teacher, Mr. Mitchell. He's so cool. Then there's this guy, Tyray, who's already sweatin' Amberlynn. I think he's a jerk, but he's really cute," Jamee went on.

Darcy ignored her, watching as more people walked out of Bluford's main doors. Finally, she spotted Hakeem at the top of the steps. Tarah and Cooper were right behind him. No one was smiling. They weren't even talking to each other.

Darcy's mouth suddenly went dry.

"Are you ready to go home?" Jamee asked. "Honestly, I don't even want to go back there. All day I kept trying to forget about what happened. I couldn't even sleep last night."

"Look, Jamee," Darcy said, trying to stay calm. She knew she should talk to her, but not now. Not with Hakeem getting closer. "Can we just talk about this later? Now isn't a good time. I'm waiting for someone."

"Well, excuse me!" Jamee said, taking a step back and looking a bit hurt. "Who are you waiting for?"

"Just go home, Jamee. I'll be there soon."

Darcy knew Cooper spotted her leaning against the fence. She saw him whisper something to Tarah, and all three of them stared and then looked away.

"Hey, here come your people, Darce," Jamee announced. "Why does everyone look so upset?"

Darcy didn't answer. Her eyes were focused on Hakeem, who stepped ahead of Cooper and slowly descended the steps. When he reached the bottom, he shook his head and put his hands out as if he was surrendering. Now was the moment she'd waited for, the time to end it with all of them. Darcy took a deep breath.

But just as she was about to speak, someone stepped in front of her.

"*There* you are," said a voice Darcy had never heard before. "I've been waiting here for ten minutes. I was startin' to wonder if I was at the wrong Bluford."

Darcy watched as a beautiful light-skinned woman in a black tank-top rushed toward Hakeem. She had close-cropped hair and wore jeans that hung low on her curvy hips, leaving part of her flat stomach exposed. She was at least three inches taller than Darcy.

The girl walked right up and gave Hakeem a hug. His arms didn't move, and his eyes turned to Darcy even as the mysterious stranger clung to his neck.

Behind him, Cooper's and Tarah's eyes were wide open. Tarah's hands pressed against her cheeks as if she was watching a car accident happen right in front of her.

"No she didn't!" Cooper said, shaking his head. "Tell me I didn't just see that, Tar."

"Oh, she did it all right," Tarah

replied somberly. "Your eyes ain't lyin'."

"*Who's that*?" Jamee asked. "And what's she doing hugging Hakeem?"

Darcy knew who it was—the girl Brisana warned her about. Everything Brisana told her was true. And what Tarah said proved to be lies. Darcy knew what she had to do.

Without a word, she walked over to Hakeem.

"What are you d-d-doing here, Anika?" Hakeem said, shifting his eyes to her and then back to Darcy. He looked like he was about to be sick to his stomach.

"I thought I'd surprise you. I got off work early, and I didn't feel like sitting in my cousin's apartment, so I thought I'd—"

"Excuse me," Darcy interrupted, tapping Anika's shoulder and glaring at Hakeem. "You need to finish this conversation some other time because Hakeem and I need to talk. *Now*."

"Who you think you are talkin' to me that way?" Anika challenged, letting go of Hakeem and turning toward her. "You don't know me."

"Darcy, look, don't do this—"

"*You're* Darcy?" Anika asked, narrowing her eyes. "I know all about you. But

66

I can see he didn't tell you about me, did he?"

Darcy's jaw dropped at the sound of her name on Anika's lips.

"Anika, *don't!*" Hakeem barked.

"Don't what?" Anika said. "You mean you didn't tell her how we met in Detroit?"

"*Stop!*"

"How you kissed me the night you gave me my first guitar lesson—"

"*Anika!*"

"Or how we e-mailed each other all summer after I moved out here? Or how you wanted to see me as soon as you got back?"

"Girl, you better shut up 'cause you're lyin' like a snake," Tarah warned, stepping right up to Anika. "Don't listen to her, Darcy. She's just tryin' to cause trouble 'cause she knows you mean more to Hakeem than she does, and she can't stand it."

"Who are *you*?" Anika asked, glaring at Tarah.

"Never mind who I am. You better start thinkin' more about who *you* are. Around here, you don't just come up spreadin' lies and talkin' to my friend like that. You ain't got no right."

"Whatever," Anika said, stepping close to Hakeem. "I ain't scared. I've seen worse then you where I come from."

Darcy felt like she had been stabbed. Each detail pushed the knife deeper, cut into the final threads that held her to Hakeem, sliced so deeply that for a second Darcy couldn't even speak.

"My cousin was right about you," Hakeem yelled, turning away from Anika and walking over to Darcy. "He said you were crazy jealous."

"*Jealous*?" Anika repeated, crossing her arms and inspecting Darcy as if she was trying to check out the damage she caused. "I just wanted her to know the truth, that's all. I mean, she does deserve that, right? Besides, I ain't stupid. I know how girls are. And I don't want her getting all confused and thinking maybe there's still something between you two."

"Darcy, it isn't like the way she's s-saying." Hakeem began to explain. "I never—"

"I don't even care anymore," Darcy cut in, unable to listen to his excuses. "Hakeem, you should have just told me about her, not snuck around at the mall so I had to hear about it from someone else. Just forget we ever had anything." Darcy turned away from him and glared at Tarah and Cooper. Anger burned like flames in her chest.

"Coop, I can almost understand where you're coming from with all this. You and Hakeem are like brothers, and you were just trying to protect him. But Tarah, what you did to me was so low I can't believe it. Don't ever call me your *girl* again, not after this. I never would've hid this from you, and I never would've thought you'd hide it from me," Darcy said, turning away from them both.

"You can keep him, Anika," Darcy continued, eyeing Hakeem for the last time. "I'm done. And if you want my advice, don't trust him or any of them."

"Darcy, c'mon, girl. You got us all wrong," Cooper protested.

Darcy ignored him. She turned and began walking home. Seconds later, she heard footsteps behind her and felt a hand on her shoulder, Hakeem's hand.

"Darcy, I'm sorry," he said.

"Don't talk to me."

"I didn't mean for things to happen this way."

"Yeah, well they did," she replied, shrugging off his hand. "I don't want to talk to you again. I'm done."

Darcy wiped her eyes and walked faster, and Hakeem let her go. In just one afternoon, she'd lost her first real boyfriend and two of her closest friends. It hurt so much she couldn't even feel the pain, like a wound so deep all the nerves were destroyed.

Even the thought of Anika didn't sting as much as it did at first. In place of pain, a cold numbness was setting in, a feeling that something inside Darcy had finally died.

Chapter 7

Just keep walking.

Darcy repeated the words to herself as she rushed away from Bluford. She wished the school and all the people she knew there could just disappear, but there was no escape, not even at home. There she'd have to deal with her parents and the questions Jamee would ask her about what just happened. She felt trapped.

Without slowing down, Darcy walked right by her house and headed straight to the cemetery where her grandparents were buried. She needed to see Grandma.

Passing through the main gates, Darcy saw an old woman place a bundle of flowers in front of a weathered headstone. She watched as the woman spoke quietly to herself and raised a tissue to her eyes. Darcy remembered a time years ago when she'd visited the cemetery with Grandma. They'd gone to put flowers at Darcy's grandfather's grave. He died of a heart attack when Darcy was five.

"The Lord works in mysterious ways, Angelcake," Grandma told her then. *"Your grandfather's been gone six years already, rest his soul. There was a time I used to say I wouldn't want to live without him. But now I see if I weren't here, I'da missed being with you, Jamee, and your mother,"* Grandma confessed as she rested flowers on the ground.

Darcy remembered the day well because it was the only time she saw her grandmother cry.

"As you get older, you start seein' that everything happens for a reason. Sometimes even the worst things turn out to be blessings in disguise. Heck, if we didn't have rain, we couldn't enjoy the sunshine, right Angelcake?" Grandma had asked her. There was a smile on her face that was both sad and beautiful at the same time, a smile Darcy could still see when she closed her eyes.

On that day, Darcy wasn't in the mood to be happy. Dad's loss was still fresh then, and it had felt like a death in the family. But Grandma's words made it a little easier, even if Darcy didn't fully believe or understand them.

If only Grandma was here now, Darcy thought as she approached the familiar granite headstone. Though it had been just a few months since Grandma passed away, the blanket of grass over her grave had already grown in so much that it nearly matched the surrounding ground. Another month, and it would blend in with the hundreds of other graves that stretched in quiet rows in the corner of the city.

Darcy sat down and ran her hand across the warm granite and traced her fingers along the words etched in the stone.

Annie Louella Duncan
Beloved
Wife   Mother   Grandmother

Birds chirped in trees overhead as Darcy began talking, telling Grandma about the trouble with her friends, the arguments with her parents, and her fears about the future.

"I just don't know what to do," she admitted, shaking her head as if

Grandma was sitting in front of her listening to every word like she used to. "It feels like everything is just falling apart, and I can't stop it. I miss you so much."

Darcy was crying softly when she suddenly heard footsteps. She quickly wiped her eyes and looked up to see Jamee. She must have followed her all the way from school. Their eyes met for a few seconds, and Darcy hoped her sister wouldn't say something stupid or expect her to talk about what happened. Jamee seemed to understand. Without a word, she sat down and put her arm on Darcy's shoulder.

The two were still for a long time before Darcy said what was on her mind, something the day's drama and the silence of Grandma's grave slowly taught her.

"We're not kids anymore," Darcy said.

Jamee nodded thoughtfully.

Maybe Jamee didn't fully understand. *Not yet*, Darcy thought. But they were the truest words Darcy could say about what had happened. Images of Mom yelling at Dad, the plate shattering on the floor, and Hakeem kissing Anika poured through her mind as she continued.

"Everything that happens from now on, *we* have to deal with it. Grandma's not here to take care of it for us. No one is," Darcy added.

"Don't forget about Mom and Dad," Jamee replied. "They're here for us . . . sort of."

Darcy glared at Jamee but didn't say anything. She knew in her mind that her parents were in trouble, that money problems and the stress of the new baby were taking a toll on them. But she didn't have the heart to tell Jamee what she was really thinking. That the days ahead were going to be difficult. That things would have to change in order for the family to survive. In the past, Grandma had stepped in and made the world right. But she was gone. Who would step up next?

Nearby a young couple placed a tiny American flag in front of a newly dug grave.

"Sometimes even the worst things turn out to be blessings in disguise."

Darcy heard Grandma's words echo in her mind, and she prayed they would be true. But as she looked to the future and thought of her friends and family, she couldn't see how.

Darcy took a deep breath as she got closer to the house. Jamee was right behind her. They had walked back from the cemetery together without a word. Darcy knew they were both wondering about the same thing.

Had Dad come home?

The house was silent when they entered. Darcy knew right away it was empty, though she could smell Dad's cologne in the air. He must have been there not long ago.

A note had been left on the kitchen counter. Spread across it were four $20 bills. Darcy pushed the money aside and picked up the note. Jamee came close to read it with her.

Mattie—I took the job at Empire Cabs. I'll be working days at the store and nights on the road. This is how we'll take care of things until I find something better. The money's yours—one night of tips. You CAN trust me.—Carl

"See, he didn't leave," Jamee said, a smile of relief on her face. "He's not going anywhere, Darce. He's just got a new job, that's all."

But Darcy's eyes were on something

else that troubled her more than any note. Next to the kitchen sink, sitting on the counter, was an empty brown beer bottle. Darcy picked it up and noticed it still contained a few drops of beer at the bottom. The sight made her head spin.

Just before Dad left years ago, he started drinking heavily. Darcy could remember the odor on his breath, the loud way he talked, the smelly beer bottles he started leaving around the house. When he first came back to the family, he told them how drinking helped him throw his life away. He'd said it again months ago when Darcy's Aunt Charlotte came over for dinner and offered him a glass of fancy wine.

"No thanks, Charlotte. I'm not touching that stuff again," he'd declared. *"Me and alcohol don't mix well."* Now he was going back on his word.

"It's not what you're thinking, Darcy," Jamee said quickly, though her face looked as if she'd seen a ghost. "I mean Dad wouldn't do that again."

"Well, what else could it be?" Darcy replied, throwing the bottle away.

"Maybe he had some friends over or something," Jamee suggested.

"Or maybe he's drinking again,"

Darcy cut back, wishing it weren't true.

Just then Darcy heard a car outside. She peered through a window to see her mother pulling up. Quickly Darcy folded up the note and put it back on the counter.

"We can't tell Mom about this," Jamee said, her eyes focused on the bottle. "She'll lose it again."

"Well, we can't just lie to her," Darcy insisted. "This is important, Jamee. She has a right to know."

Jamee looked out the window and rubbed her forehead as if she were in pain.

"Look, Darcy. Don't go crazy. This isn't new. I've found a few of them—"

"*What?!* And you never said anything?" Darcy yelled, unable to believe her ears. She remembered the bottle on the steps last night and Dad's late night walks. He *had* been drinking again. Not only had her friends been keeping secrets, but her own sister had too. "How could you hide something like that from us after all he did?"

"I knew you'd flip out, that's why. You'd go crazy, and Mom would act like it's the end of the world and things would just get worse around here. Look, it's not a big deal. It's just beer," Jamee replied, avoiding Darcy's stare.

"If it's not a big deal, you wouldn't be keeping it a secret from me or Mom," Darcy said.

Jamee hid the bottle deep in the trash can.

"You're trying to protect Dad, aren't you? You're always on his side."

"No, it's not that," Jamee paused, struggling for words. "I'm trying to protect *us*, Darcy. I just want things to be okay. No more screaming and yelling, you know? If Mom finds out about this, I'm scared what she'll do. I'm scared of what will happen."

Darcy knew Jamee meant what she said. But the idea of lying to her mother seemed so wrong. Outside, a heavy car door slammed. Mom would be walking through the door in seconds.

"I'm scared too, Jamee, but if you have to lie just to keep the peace, what's the point? I mean what kinda family are we if the only thing that holds us together is a lie?"

Jamee shook her head. "Please don't tell her, Darcy," she said, desperation in her voice, as if she was begging. "Don't do it. *Please.*"

79

The front door opened then, and Darcy heard heavy footsteps moving closer.

"Girls? Carl? Anyone here?"

Darcy could hear the weariness in her mother's voice.

"We're in the kitchen, Mom," Darcy said.

Across from her, Jamee shook her head. "Don't do it," she whispered.

Darcy took a deep breath and tried to think of a gentle way to tell the truth just as her mother stepped into the kitchen.

"Did your father call?" Mom asked, walking slowly toward the counter. Darcy knew by the way she moved that her feet were sore and her back was aching. "Did either of you see him?"

Darcy looked at Jamee and then at Mom. For a second she couldn't speak as she stared at the dark circles beneath her mother's eyes and the wrinkles that stretched across her forehead. If it were possible, Darcy could swear Mom had aged five years since she saw her this morning.

"I didn't see him, but he left a note," Darcy answered finally. Jamee handed Mom the note along with the money.

Mom read it, took a deep breath and

sighed. For a second, she looked as if she was about to collapse with relief.

"Everything's okay, Mom," Jamee said. "He was just at work, that's all."

"He's a stubborn man, but I guess I can't fault him for trying to do the right thing," Mom said, rereading the note and putting the money in her pocket. "I don't want him driving a cab in the middle of the night, but I was wrong to come down so hard on him, and I was wrong to put you two in the middle of it. I'm sorry," she confessed, looking more exhausted than ever.

"And Jamee . . ." Without another word, Mom embraced Jamee and whispered something in her ear. The two hugged quietly, and then Mom reached an arm around Darcy. "What would I do without you two?" she sighed.

Darcy glanced at Jamee's tears and then at her mother's tired face. There was no way she could tell her about the beer bottle hidden nearby. Sure, it was a lie, and by keeping silent she was adding to it. But it seemed crueler to tell Mom the truth in such a state. Doing so would shatter her like a piece of glass.

But Dad's secret couldn't last forever. Her mind turned to her own friends and how just hours ago the truth tore them all to pieces. Dad's problem would do the same thing to her family.

"Everything okay with you girls today?" Mom asked. "I got so caught up, I forgot to ask you about your first day of school."

"I had the greatest first day, Mom," Jamee said, explaining all the details Darcy had already heard.

Mom yawned and rubbed her temples when Jamee finished. She turned to Darcy then. "And what about you?" she said. "I bet it was great seeing Hakeem and the rest of the gang again."

Darcy couldn't raise her eyes or look at her mother's face. In her mind, she thought of the new baby resting in Mom's belly. She knew the truth would destroy everything. And a simple lie could give them all peace, at least for a little while.

"It was nice, Mom," Darcy said finally, deciding to keep the peace for another day. "Just like old times," she added, escaping down the dark hallway to her room alone.

Chapter 8

It was pitch-black when Darcy heard the sounds. First a thud of footsteps as someone walked into the kitchen. Then the "thunk" of the heavy refrigerator door followed by the quick hiss and snap of a beer bottle opening.

It was Dad. He must have just come home from a night of work. Darcy crept out of her bed and into the hallway. She wasn't going to let him drink again.

As she reached the kitchen, she noticed it was empty and dark. Confused, she took a step forward and felt a stinging pain in her foot. She reached down and felt something sharp sticking from her heel. She could feel wetness on her fingers too. Something warm was dripping off her foot.

Blood.

In a panic, she hopped to the bathroom to grab a towel, but when she got there, the bathroom counter was empty except for a single beer bottle glistening in the dark. Darcy turned on the light and noticed her foot then. A shard of broken china stabbed deep into her heel. The gash it opened was as long as her thumb.

"Mom! Dad! I cut myself bad, and I'm bleeding," she cried.

No one answered. They must be asleep, she thought.

"Mom! Dad! Jamee?!" Darcy yelled out again. Her blood was spilling onto the floor in thick red drops.

In the mirror, Darcy saw her reflection. A frightened girl holding her bloody foot stared back at her. She looked desperate. Alone. Almost childlike. But then Darcy saw other faces in the mirror.

Anika's angry glare.

Cooper, Tarah, and Hakeem laughing at her.

Her parents in tears yelling at her.

And Brian Mason. He seemed to reach at her from the mirror, his hand piercing through it as if it were water.

"No!" She screamed.

The mirror exploded into a shower of glass that rained down in jagged pieces *falling toward her face.*

"No!"

Darcy bolted upright in her bed covered in a layer of sweat, her heart pounding like a drum. She reached down to her foot. Her heel was fine. No blood. No broken plate. Darcy sighed and looked at her clock. It was 5:17 in the morning.

She laid back and looked at the ceiling, dreading the day ahead.

"What am I gonna do?" she whispered into the dark.

In her mind, she kept seeing herself in the mirror. A scared lonely girl. It may have been a dream, but she knew part of it was real. The events of the past days had left her more alone than ever. Cut off from her family. Her ex-boyfriend. Even her best friend.

"You don't just drop your people," Tarah had said. *"When stuff happens, which it always does, you work through it . . . it's what you gotta do when somethin's important."*

Darcy felt as if she was the one who'd been dropped. Everyone had let her down somehow, walked away from her, lied to her. Betrayed her.

But alone in the darkness of her quiet

bedroom, part of her knew it wasn't that simple. She had cut off Tarah, not the other way around. And she had done other things too. Kept her secrets about Brian hidden from Hakeem, lied to Mom about her first day at school, hid the news about the beer bottle from her.

That's different, she thought to herself.

Sure, she'd lied. But she did it to keep the peace. To keep everyone happy. To keep things from flying apart like the mirror in her dream. Telling the truth would have shattered everything. Darcy had lied for the right reasons.

But what if Tarah felt the same way? What if she lied for the same reasons? The questions made Darcy's head spin. She flipped onto her side, unable to get comfortable.

"We're not kids anymore," she whispered to herself. The words she'd spoken at Grandma's grave seemed truer than ever. When Darcy was younger, the world was simpler and easier somehow. Things were either right or wrong. Good or bad.

But now everything was mixed and messy, full of cracks and broken pieces like the mirror in her dreams.

Darcy sat up in her bed, giving up on

sleep. She couldn't stop her mind from racing through everything that had happened. Her thoughts still went back to Tarah, the person whose actions hurt her most.

"*You don't lie to your friends,*" Darcy wanted to say. "*I trusted you.*"

"*You don't drop your friends,*" would be Tarah's reply. "*I'm one of them.*"

It was a voice Darcy couldn't completely ignore, even though she wanted to. Tired and frustrated, she stretched and dragged herself out of bed.

Outside, the dark was giving way to the coming dawn, and Darcy could see the dim outlines of pictures she'd hung on the wall opposite her bed. There were two old photos of Hakeem, a picture of Cooper and Tarah, and a snapshot of all four of them at the beach.

She hadn't taken them down.

Not yet.

Two hours later, Darcy headed out the front door with Jamee. Unlike yesterday, she hoped her sister would walk to Bluford without her, but Jamee didn't cooperate. Instead, she'd waited while Darcy packed her bookbag, and then she rushed out the door the instant

87

Darcy decided to leave.

Darcy was not in the mood for her or Bluford as they turned up the block toward the high school. Just a few doors from their house, Darcy spotted a brown beer bottle. The sight of it left a queasy feeling in the pit of her stomach. They still had to deal with Dad.

"Me and Dez got in a fight last night on the phone," Jamee said, glancing quickly at the bottle and then at Darcy. "It was about you."

"*Me?*" Darcy replied. The last thing she wanted to think about was Jamee and her boyfriend, Cooper's little brother, arguing about her. "Don't you two have something better to talk about?"

"I'm serious, Darce. He told me Coop and Tarah are really upset about what happened yesterday. I said it serves them right, they should be upset for what they did. But he got mad at me, sayin' we were both overreacting," Jamee explained.

"First of all, it's none of *his* business—or yours. You shouldn't have been there, Jamee. And second, I don't need any fourteen-year-old telling me what to do, especially not Coop's brother. What does he know anyway?" Darcy snapped.

"That's what *I* said. Now that we're at Bluford, he's been actin' all weird. I got so mad at him last night, we practically broke up," Jamee said as they crossed a street together. "I know it's not any of my business, but I just gotta say I think you were right about what you told everybody yesterday. If I were you, I'da lost it and started hitting somebody. Especially that girl huggin' Hakeem."

Darcy winced at her sister's words. Even though she meant well, Jamee was practically rubbing in what had happened.

"Thanks," Darcy said, hoping Jamee would drop the subject and talk about something else.

"Cindy and Amberlynn totally agree . . . I mean, about my fight with Dez," Jamee said quickly, her eyes suddenly darting away.

Darcy could a feel a headache building behind her eyes. Even though Jamee didn't exactly admit it, Darcy knew she'd told her friends everything about Hakeem. The private details of her relationship were now freshman gossip. People she didn't even know were already talking about how some strange girl from Detroit had ripped her boyfriend away. Darcy was about to scream at Jamee when something caught her eye, a sight that made her heart jump into her throat.

A red Toyota with oversized tires and chrome rims waited at a traffic light. It sat low on its wide wheels, just inches from the ground. It was a car Darcy knew well, one she'd even gone to the beach in months ago when Hakeem left.

No.

It can't be.

He's supposed to be gone, hundreds of miles away. That's what his sister told her after the attack. But the Toyota up the street looked every bit like Brian Mason's.

Darcy stood frozen on the sidewalk, watching the car turn a corner and disappear. Her mouth was suddenly dry, and she could hear ringing in her ears. A tremor raced down her back.

Relax, she thought, trying to stay calm. *Be realistic. Maybe he sold his car. Maybe someone else tricked out a Toyota so it looked exactly like his. There could be hundreds of cars just like it on the road*, Darcy tried to convince herself.

"Are you okay?" Jamee asked, breaking Darcy's thoughts. "You look like you saw a ghost or something."

Darcy took a deep breath and tried to hide that her hands were cold and trembling. At least Jamee hadn't seen the car and figured out what it meant. At least that story would not be part of Bluford's gossip. Not yet anyway.

"I'm fine," Darcy said, forcing herself to walk forward. "I don't want you or your friends talking about me or Hakeem anymore, okay?"

"Yeah, whatever," Jamee said, eying Darcy carefully. "What is it? Why are you so upset all the sudden?"

Darcy knew Jamee sensed something was wrong, but she wasn't about to tell her the truth.

"I told you, *I'm fine*," Darcy repeated, stepping ahead of her sister.

But as they approached the lot outside of Bluford, Darcy was sure her biggest secret had come back to haunt her.

Brian Mason had returned.

Darcy still felt lightheaded at lunchtime. But she forced herself to focus on her morning classes.

Chemistry had been the most difficult with Tarah nearby. The two didn't say a word the entire period, though at several points Darcy wanted to turn around and talk to her. She could almost sense that Tarah felt the same way, though neither could find the words. Darcy wasn't even sure what they were anymore.

As Tarah walked out of class, she dropped a folded piece of paper on Darcy's desk. Darcy recognized Hakeem's scratchy handwriting immediately. She read the note once in class and then again while she waited for Brisana at their lunch table.

Dear Darcy,

I am SO sorry about yesterday. I'm even more sorry for never telling you about Anika. I was afraid if you learned the truth, you'd be hurt. But now I've hurt you more.

You deserve the truth, so here it is. I was so depressed in Detroit without you. Anika was my neighbor. I met her one night when I was playing my guitar. We liked each other right away. We hung out a few times, and we kissed. But that's ALL that happened. I swear.

The girl has problems. She ended up leaving Detroit, and I thought that was the last I'd see her. Then she wrote and told me she was living with her cousin an hour from here. I'm being straight up, Darcy. We e-mailed each other all summer. I promised I'd meet her if I ever got back. That's what happened on Saturday. I had no idea she was going to show up yesterday.

I should've told you all this sooner, but I was scared. And to be honest, I'm confused. The reason I started seeing Anika was because we were apart. I never thought I'd see you again, but here I am. Yesterday reminded me of how much we had. It seems wrong to let it all go. But I understand if that's what you want.

No matter what, I'm sorry. Maybe we can go to Niko's again, just you and me? Let me know.

> She stares at me, her eyes onyx fire.
> I burn in them. I've been a liar.
> What I did was a dumb mistake.
> What we had shouldn't break.
> If I could do it over again,
> I'd fix it all. There'd be no end.

Love, Hak

"What's that?" Brisana asked, sitting down at the table with her usual salad. Her eyes were focused on the paper in Darcy's shaking hands.

"It's a note from Hakeem," Darcy admitted, slipping it into her notebook.

"What's *he* want?"

"I'm not sure. Maybe a second chance," Darcy replied, her head spinning with the news and the answer she knew she had to give him.

"*Please*! Don't tell me you're going to take him back, not after what he did with that girl," Brisana said. She looked as if she had just tasted something sour in her salad.

Darcy didn't say a word. Instead, she grabbed a piece of paper and wrote a short reply back to Hakeem. She dropped it on Tarah's table without a word just before the lunch period ended. She knew it would get to Hakeem right away.

She'd written just four words to him.
"Meet me after school."

Chapter 9

Hakeem was already outside when Darcy headed out of Bluford. She saw him pacing at the bottom of the steps where she had been the day before.

What a difference a day makes, Darcy thought to herself as she approached. She was still angry at him, but she had to put an end to the lies. He'd dumped his secrets, but hers were still gnawing at her.

She'd given up on getting back together with him. But she knew she'd never be able to clear her head unless she told him what really happened. Only then would she free herself from the guilt about lying to him. Only then could she look at him and know she'd done the right thing. With him or without him, it was the only way she could move on.

And it had to happen now.

"Hi, Darcy," Hakeem said, his voice wavering slightly. She could tell he was fighting his stutter.

"Let's go to the park," she said, avoiding his nervous gaze. "There's something I need to tell you."

He nodded, and they walked several blocks without a word. In her mind, Darcy tried to rehearse what she'd say, but everything was jumbled. They crossed into the park where they once walked hand-in-hand. Only now they kept their distance, careful not to touch. She led him to a bench and sat down.

"Darcy, I just want to say this one more time. I'm sorry—"

"I don't want you to say anything else until you hear what I've got to tell you," she said, cutting him off. Each of his apologies added to the guilt pressing down on her. She needed him to stop until he'd heard everything. Then he'd have a choice to make. So would she.

"If he's the person I think he is, he'll handle it just right," Tarah had said. *"If not, you're better off without him."* Now was the time to find out.

"What is it, Darcy?" he asked.

"When you were away, I started seeing

someone too," she said.

Hakeem's brown eyes opened wide. *"What?"*

Without pausing, Darcy told him how she'd met Brian, how he'd comforted her when Hakeem left. She even mentioned their walks on the beach and how she'd kissed him. But she held back the rest of the truth, the part about the attack. It was her darkest secret, a knot of shame and hurt she still wasn't sure she could tell.

Hakeem's face looked pained, as if he was squinting at the sun or something, but his eyes were aimed down at the ground.

"Why didn't you tell me about him? You should have told me, Darcy," he said, kicking his heels against the edge of their bench.

"And you should have told me about Anika before I saw her hugging you," Darcy cut back.

Hakeem shook his head. Darcy knew what he was feeling. Hurt and jealousy, the sour mix that made her want to scream yesterday.

"I'm not gonna lie, Darcy. I don't like thinking about you with someone else. It hurts me right here," he said, slapping his chest. "But what can I say? We broke up. I couldn't expect you to just stop living after I left. What kinda person would I be if I did that?"

Hakeem stared at her then. His eyes seemed to gaze right into her, and Darcy had to look away. He was showing himself to be what she remembered, what led her to him in the first place. He was smart, kind, friendly, and deep. He was trying his best to be straight up with her. She knew how hard that was. She still hadn't managed to be straight up with him. The secrets she'd hidden for so long were falling away, but the biggest one still remained.

Darcy turned back and noticed the park was completely empty. Everything seemed still and tense. Even the birds grew quiet, and the sun hung like a giant red eye staring down at them. She braced herself for what she had to say next, the secret that hurt her the most and haunted her even this morning as she watched the Toyota pull up the street.

"There's something else, Hakeem. Something I always wanted to hide from you, but I can't anymore," she said.

Hakeem massaged his forehead and

temples like he had a headache, but then he shook off whatever pained him, sat upright, took a deep breath, and focused on her. "You can tell me anything, Darcy."

"Something happened with Brian," she admitted, struggling for the words she knew she had to say. "I mean nothing *really* happened, but it almost did. My father stopped everything, but before that Brian almost . . . I mean things just got—"

"What is it, Darcy? What are you trying to say?"

"We were kissing on his couch. I shouldn't have even been there. I was so stupid, but he seemed so nice, and I was missing you," Darcy explained, unable to look in Hakeem's eyes.

"What happened? What did he do?" Hakeem asked, his voice rising with concern and anger.

"He wouldn't stop," Darcy answered. Her words seemed to freeze the entire park. For several seconds, nothing moved. Not the ants on the ground. Not the leaves in the trees. Not even cars on the street nearby.

"*What?!*"

Darcy couldn't raise her head to look

at Hakeem, but she couldn't hold back the truth either. "I asked him to stop, but he just kept pushing me, you know? I got so scared. If my dad hadn't come over, I don't know what would have happened," she explained. She even told him about the nightmares, how Tarah helped her, and the scare she had on the way to Bluford.

That's when she realized Hakeem wasn't okay. He was sitting with his arms crossed and his legs twitching with nervous energy. His face was bunched up in an angry scowl.

"Tarah knew about this and didn't tell me?" he asked, not waiting for an answer. "I can't believe it. Y'all are supposed to be my friends. If something serious happens, I should know about it," he protested.

"It wasn't her secret to tell. It was mine, and I would have never forgiven her if she told you. She was just protecting me, that's all."

"*Protecting you?!* It don't seem like anyone's been doing that since I left. Where is this punk? Dude needs to learn a lesson," Hakeem yelled.

"No, Hakeem. This was months ago. It's over—"

"It's not over, Darcy! You can't just drop this on me and expect me to be cool with it," Hakeem cut back. He stood up from the bench and started pacing in front of her like a caged lion. "That punk coulda hurt you."

"Calm down!" Darcy said, moving into his path and putting her hands on his chest. "I'm okay. Nothing really happened."

"No, something *did* happen. I can't believe this is the first time I'm hearing about it. It's been months! Someone should have told me."

Darcy knew the feeling well. His words were the same as hers yesterday. And her reasons for hiding the truth weren't much different from his.

"I was scared of what you'd think about me," Darcy admitted. "Like maybe you'd blame me for what happened." She'd heard guys talk. She knew the ugly words they had for girls, especially one who went to a guy's apartment alone. Darcy hated the words and knew they were wrong, but Hakeem might not. She always feared he'd think less of her for what happened.

"*Blame you?* You didn't do this. The sorry coward who pushed you around is

101

the one I blame. I need to talk to him," Hakeem fumed, his eyes flashing with anger. He suddenly looked scary, his face hard and mean.

Darcy stepped back. She wasn't sure what to say to calm him down. She'd only wanted him to understand what happened. She hadn't expected him to flip out.

"There's nothing you need to say to him. It's done," Darcy replied.

"Coop know about this too?" he asked, ignoring her comment.

Darcy wasn't sure of the answer. Tarah was the only one who knew and could have told Cooper. But the more Darcy learned, the more she thought Tarah had kept her secret.

"It ain't right for me to be tellin' everybody's secrets, especially when the secrets can hurt people," Tarah had said. Darcy believed her.

"I don't think so," she answered. "Why?"

Hakeem turned away from her suddenly. "Look, Darcy. I gotta go. I'll call you later."

"Where are you going?" she called. She didn't like the stormy look on his face, the tightness in his jaw. "Hakeem?"

He didn't look back or slow down. Instead, he headed out of the park and back into the streets.

"Everything'll be all right," he called out as he left. "I just need to take a walk, that's all. I'll call you."

As she watched him walk away, Darcy wasn't sure exactly where Hakeem was going. But inside she knew what he was going to find once he got there— trouble.

Darcy rushed home unsure what to do.

Her mother was walking out the door when Darcy turned the corner onto their street. Mom was wearing her hospital ID badge as she slowly made her way to the car.

Darcy could see her mother was exhausted. But as she got closer, Darcy thought Mom looked even worse. Her face was gray and puffy. She almost looked sick, like she was fighting the flu or something.

"Where you going, Mom? Aren't you supposed to be taking nights off from now on?" Darcy asked.

Mom sat down slowly in the car as if her back was sore.

"Don't start lecturing me. I got enough of that from your sister. I don't need it from you too," Mom snapped. "Someone called out at the hospital, so I'm gonna fill in. They're gonna pay me overtime, and Lord knows we need the money if we're ever gonna afford this baby."

"Can't you let someone else go in?" Darcy asked. "You can't work like this. You're too tired."

Jamee walked outside. She must have heard them talking.

"That's enough from both of you. I'm going to work, and that's it. Even with his new job, your father's gonna have to work eighty hours a week to keep us above water once the baby's born. The more we can save up before then, the better. Now I'm sorry. You might not like it, but that's the way it's gonna have to be," Mom explained.

But Mom, Darcy wanted to say, *Dad's drinking again and you're the only one who doesn't see it. He's not going to be able to hold up under all that pressure.* Yet Darcy couldn't say a word even as she checked for beer bottles on the front step. There were none.

"Now I'll be back late, so don't wait up

for me. Your father said he was getting off early tonight. He should be back around ten. There's leftovers in the fridge," she explained, putting the car into gear.

"We're gonna have to tell her the truth, Jamee," Darcy said as soon as their mother pulled away. "We can't keep lying to her."

Jamee nodded somberly. "I found where he's hiding the beer. There's a cooler hidden in the crawl space under the house. I found a bottle cap in the backyard and saw this little panel that he pried open. I couldn't believe it."

Neither could Darcy until Jamee led her to a spot in their tiny backyard. Just as Jamee described, there was a thin metal panel right above the ground. Jamee pulled it away to reveal a blue cooler not much bigger than Darcy's bookbag. Inside were four bottles exactly like the empty one she'd found in the kitchen. Darcy shook her head in shock. Her father had been hiding his problem right underneath them.

"Maybe that's why he wanted this house," Jamee said bitterly. "Because he knew it had a hiding spot." Her voice was heavy with sadness, as if the image she had of her father had been shattered forever.

"We have to tell Mom about this tonight, Jamee," Darcy said, putting the panel back in place. She wanted her mother to see it for herself. "As soon as she gets home."

A tear rolled down Jamee's face. "I'm scared of what's gonna happen."

"Me too," Darcy said, giving her a hug. "Me too."

A few hours later, Darcy's cell phone rang. Her heart jumped in her chest.

The moment she'd watched Hakeem storm out of the park, she felt something bad would happen. She was so sure she'd even tried to call Tarah and Cooper, but neither was home. She even thought about calling the police but then talked herself out of it.

What if you're wrong? What if he just needed to clear his head? She thought.

One thing that made her feel better was that no one had called her with bad news. Everything had been quiet. Until now.

She looked at the phone and saw that the call was from Tarah's house.

"Hello?"

"Hey girl. It's me," Tarah said. Darcy could hear the worry in her voice. "Look, I know we got lots to talk about, but somethin' serious is happenin', and I'm scared."

"What is it, Tarah?" Darcy asked, even though she already knew the answer.

"It's Coop and Hakeem. They're goin' after Brian. We gotta stop 'em before they do somethin' stupid."

Chapter 10

Darcy ran out of her house onto the dark street.

"Where you goin'? It's gettin' late," Jamee asked.

"Don't worry about it. I'll be back soon," Darcy yelled as she headed down the block. She knew she had to move quick. Tarah told her that Cooper and Hakeem left ten minutes ago. That meant they'd be at Brian's any second if they weren't there already.

"I ain't never seen Hakeem so upset," Tarah had explained. "He got all in my face for not tellin' him what happened to you. Coop tried to calm him down and that's when Hakeem told *him* what Brian did. Next thing I know, they're both racin' off in Coop's truck. You gotta do something, Darce. You're the only one who can stop this now."

Darcy didn't know what she'd do as she raced to the corner and sprinted toward Brian's apartment building four blocks away. Tarah's house was on the other side of the neighborhood, a ten-minute drive. There was no time for her to get involved, Darcy knew that. She had to handle this on her own.

People on the sidewalk glared at her as she darted between them and plowed ahead. On one corner, a car skidded loudly as she dashed into the street. On another block, someone shouted a curse at her, but she didn't care. Her friends' lives were at stake.

A police car rolled by up ahead. Darcy was about to flag it down, but it sped off before she had a chance. She was only two blocks away.

Even at that distance, she could see the cement walls of the apartment building up ahead. Her eyes scanned up to the fourth floor window of the Masons' apartment. The lights were on.

The sight made her stomach tighten up like a fist. She could picture the inside of the apartment. The family pictures on the wall. The glass coffee table. The sofa where Brian pinned her.

The memory still filled her with an anger no words could describe. An anger that didn't fade as the weeks and months passed. An anger at guys who hurt others, who ignore it when a girl says *no*.

"Yo, take it easy. I don't see no fire," a man shouted as Darcy raced down the last block. She'd nearly hit him as she flew by.

Darcy heard someone yelling as she reached the parking lot next to the building. She turned and spotted Cooper's old pick-up truck. Its doors were open, its engine idling loudly. Next to it was a red Toyota.

This time Darcy was sure it was Brian's car.

In the beam of the truck's headlights, she saw Brian. He was wearing a loose black T-shirt and baggy jeans. A grease stain was on his pants as if he had been working on his car. Hakeem was in front of him, his face inches from Brian's. Cooper was right beside him.

"You think you're a man?" Hakeem growled. "I'm about to teach you what a man is right now."

"No!" Darcy yelled from across the lot, but no one seemed to hear her voice.

110

Hakeem lunged at Brian, sending two quick punches to his face, one to his chin, the other to his cheek. Darcy could hear the heavy blows landing as she rushed closer.

"No!" she screamed again, but the fight possessed them. She watched as Brian shoved Hakeem back and punched the side of his face, his knuckles hitting with a loud crack. She'd crossed the parking lot, stopping just a few feet away.

Cooper circled close like a shark ready to strike. Brian, struggling against Hakeem, was defenseless against him. Cooper's punches would not be blocked.

But Darcy didn't want it. She never asked for her friends to do this. She never wanted to see them risk their lives and futures for her, or waste them on a piece of trash like Brian.

"*Stop it!*" she ordered. Her voice couldn't be louder, but the boys struggled, cursing and punching like animals. Drops of blood stained Hakeem's shirt. Cooper's fists were raised like two hammers ready to destroy Brian.

Darcy knew she had to act.

"I said *stop it!*" she yelled, stepping right in front of Cooper. His eyes

111

widened at the sight of her, as if she had suddenly broken the spell he'd been under. He lowered his fists and backed up. "Help me break this up, Coop," she ordered.

Cooper shook his head like she'd asked him to do something impossible. Darcy cursed and rushed to Hakeem, pushing against him with all her might, trying to separate him from Brian. "Don't do this. He's not worth it," she screamed.

"Watch out!"

Darcy heard Cooper's warning, but her back was to Brian. She had just enough time to brace herself.

Whap!

She felt as if a bullet ripped into her back, though there was no gunshot. She knew it was Brian's fist that struck her from behind. The blow made her legs buckle but not fall.

She heard Cooper yelling something, but she focused on Hakeem, blocking out the pain. She stared into his eyes with something she hadn't felt in months. She wanted to stop him, to calm him, to protect him.

"Look at me!" she commanded, putting her hands on his face. *"Look at me!"*

Finally she saw the anger in his eyes begin to melt. Saw that he recognized her. She latched onto his shoulders even as he tried to shrug her off.

"What are you doin' here, Darcy?" he asked. "This ain't the place for you."

"It's not the place for you either. He's not worth it," she said.

"I ain't scared of either of you," Brian growled behind her. "Y'all just a couple of little boys."

Darcy turned to see Cooper and Brian circling each other. Cooper had shoved Brian back, kept him away from Darcy and Hakeem. He was protecting them, though he looked like he wanted to do more. She knew Hakeem wanted to too, but she got their attention. She forced them to pause. To think.

"And you're nothing but a coward who pushes girls around," she snapped back, walking over to him. It was the first time she faced him since the attack. But after the counseling and the fight, he seemed smaller somehow. Nothing like the Brian in her dreams.

"What you did to me was wrong, and you know it. Part of me wants to see you hurt, but then I'd be just like you. Now if you were really a man, you'd step up, apologize and learn how to treat people. But I'm not holding my breath for that," she said, turning to Hakeem and Cooper. "My friends may be younger, but they're more man than you'll ever be."

Brian rolled his eyes, but Darcy didn't care. She was done with him. The nightmare of the beginning of the summer was over. She'd stood up to the monster and stared it down. But there were bigger monsters at home. She looked at her watch and realized Dad would be home in less than an hour.

"You are either crazy or the bravest girl I know," Cooper said as they walked away together back to his truck. "I ain't sure which yet."

"She's both," Hakeem said, putting his arm on Darcy's shoulder and turning to her. They stopped walking. "I'm sorry I wasn't here to protect you. I'm so sorry," he said, his voice wavering. He hugged her then, the truest embrace he'd ever given. For the first time since he'd been back, she felt glimmers of the past, a feeling of connection, of understanding, of honesty.

"I don't need you to protect me," she replied.

"She's right," Cooper chimed in from

his truck. "Maybe we need her to protect us. I can't wait to tell Tarah about all this."

"I got a few things I need to tell her too, Coop," Darcy said. She knew now that Tarah had been loyal to her all along, that she'd been in an impossible situation and did the best she could. It was all Darcy could ask of anyone. When she got a chance, she'd apologize. But not tonight.

Not with what waited in store for her.

Jamee was on the phone when Darcy walked in.

"*He's not there?*" she said into the phone. "Well, where is he? I was told he was getting off around ten." Jamee's eyes suddenly grew wide. She hung up the phone without saying goodbye.

"What is it? What's wrong?" Darcy asked.

"I'm trying to find Dad. The cab company said he had off today. But Mom said he was working tonight."

"Huh?"

"Don't you get it, Darcy? He lied to Mom. He's probably off drinking somewhere," Jamee said, sitting down on the couch and putting her face in her

115

hands. "After you left, Mom called. She hurt her back at work and needs a ride home. She didn't have Dad's new work number, so she asked me to call him. But he's not there. I don't know what to do. Everything's falling apart." Jamee's last words broke into gentle sobs.

Darcy looked at the clock. It was almost ten. She was about to call Cooper to ask for a ride when she heard a car pull up. She peeked out the window and saw Dad.

"He's here," Darcy said, feeling her hands tremble with nervous energy.

"If he's drunk, Darcy, I swear to God I will lose it," Jamee said.

Dad walked in a second later. Darcy and Jamee watched in icy silence as he took off his jacket. There was nothing unusual about the way he moved. If he drank anything, it wasn't much, Darcy thought.

"What's wrong with you two?" he asked as soon as he came into the living room. His eyes were on Jamee. It was clear she'd been crying.

"Mom called," Darcy said, "She hurt her back and needs a ride home. *Now.*"

"What happened?" Dad asked, his eyes widened with alarm. "Is she okay?"

"What do you care?" Jamee snapped. "If you were so concerned, you wouldn't have lied about where you were tonight."

Darcy watched as her father nodded and took a long, sad breath.

"Let's go get your mother. We'll talk when we know she's okay. I have a lot to tell you." He grabbed the keys he'd just put down and headed out the door.

Jamee flashed Darcy a look. She was giving up on Dad with every second, and it was tearing her apart inside. Darcy could read it on her sister's face.

Darcy felt it too. Their family was a ship that was slowly sinking under the sea.

Dad raced to the hospital. No one talked during the car ride, but they rushed out together and headed straight to the emergency room where Mom worked. Inside, the air smelled of floor cleanser and body odor.

In the hallway outside the ER, an entire family sat looking pale with worry. Inside, Darcy nearly collided with a middle-aged woman standing beside an old man in a wheelchair. He coughed loudly as Darcy passed. A horrible gurgling sound came from his lungs.

How can Mom spend so much time here? Darcy wondered.

Dad spoke to a doctor and was directed to a small office area just around the corner from the emergency room. Mom was there stretched out on a portable hospital bed. She looked like a patient, not a nurse.

"What happened, Mattie?" Dad asked, rushing to her side.

"I can't do it no more, Carl. My back gave out," Mom said. Darcy could see she had been crying too. Her eyes still glistened with tears. "Doctor tells me I gotta slow down or I'm gonna hurt myself and the baby."

"Then you better listen," Dad said. "That's what we've been telling you."

"But you're gonna have to work two jobs to make up for my lost overtime. Don't lie to me, Carl. You can't work that much. No one can," Mom said shaking her head sadly.

"We'll figure it out, Mattie," Dad said, glancing back at Darcy and Jamee. "You just have to have faith. I'm leaning on that a lot these days."

Jamee wept softly and leaned into Darcy. The ship was still sinking. Darcy could feel it slide, and she couldn't stand it. There had to be something more she could do than just watch it happen.

"You can lean on me too," Darcy said suddenly.

"Huh?" Everyone turned to her.

"I've been thinking about it for a long time, and I've decided to work more. I know I can work twenty-five hours a week and still keep up my grades—"

"No, I won't let you do that," Mom said.

"It's what I'm gonna do, Mom," Darcy replied. It was true. She wouldn't take no for an answer.

"But—"

"Listen, Mom. I'm older now, and this is what I want to do. If my grades slip, I'll cut back. But if not, why shouldn't I work?"

"No, it's not right. We don't want to be a burden to you—"

"But we're family, Mom. That's what we do for each other. You and Grandma taught us that. Besides, I am that baby's big sister," Darcy added. "It's time for you to let me be that."

"I can help too. I can babysit for extra money," Jamee offered then. "I know it's not much, but it's something. I'm going to be a big sister too."

Mom shook her head at her two daughters. "When did you two get so stubborn?" she asked.

"They take after you," Dad said, gently rubbing Mom's shoulder. He leaned back and looked at the girls, his own eyes glistening with tears of pride. "You and your mother."

At home, Mom went to her room immediately, and Dad sat up with the girls in the living room.

"I'm going to treat you like adults because you acted like adults tonight," Dad announced. "You can tell your mother now or later. I haven't told her because I didn't want to upset her with the baby, but I'll let you decide after you hear everything."

Darcy was hanging on his every word. She knew what was at stake. Would they survive as a family or not? Dad took a deep breath.

"You're right, Jamee. I wasn't at work tonight. I was at a meeting for people like me. People with drinking problems. It's called Alcoholics Anonymous. I used to go to these meetings all the time, but I got better and stopped going. With all the stress, I started drinking again. Nothing serious, but I realized it could become a problem, so I got help. This week, I started going to the meetings everyday. Being a cabby allows me to do that," he admitted.

"See this?" he said, holding up a small coin with a prayer on it. "This is a token I have to keep me from drinking. Your words tonight, your faces right now, that baby on the way. I've got plenty of reasons not to drink, and I swear I will work everyday to make sure I don't. You girls, your mom, this family, are the most precious things in the world to me. I will not throw that away again. *Never*," Dad promised.

Darcy wiped her eyes as her father finished speaking. His words were pure and true, and she could see he believed them with all his heart. Jamee wrapped her arms around him, and Darcy embraced them both. They barely even noticed Mom standing at the edge of the living room listening to every word. She quietly joined them in the embrace, their tears flowing together.

They were still a family. A stronger family than Darcy realized.

"*Sometimes even the worst things*

turn out to be blessings in disguise." Grandma's words seemed truer now than ever. At several points over the past few days, Darcy was sure her family and friendships were coming to an end, and her world would be forever broken. Now Darcy realized she had been wrong. Many things had changed, but nothing was destroyed.

Mom's tiredness forced her to get the rest she and the baby needed. Dad's problem actually brought him closer to the family, showed everyone the love and commitment he had made to them. And the stress of the past few days had also changed Darcy.

She was different than she'd been just a week ago. Older somehow. Wiser. Less scared. It was true she was not a child anymore. The events of the past week and the afternoon at Grandma's grave taught her that. But in place of the child she had been was something greater. Something more powerful.

A budding adult. A young woman.

Sure, she would now have to work harder, take more responsibility, help out her family more. Darcy knew that. But she also knew she joined a line of powerful women who had done that before her. Her mother and her grand-mother.

Now it was Darcy's turn. She felt honored to be in such company.

At 6:30 a.m., Darcy was awakened by a strange sound. A scratching noise. It was coming from the backyard. She bolted upright in her bed.

Please God. Don't let it be what I think it is.

Darcy ran to the window and looked out. Standing there alone in the yellow dawn was her father. He was pulling beer bottles from the crawl space, opening them and pouring them gently into the grass.

Thank you, God.

She heard him tossing the bottles one-by-one into a trash can. Heard them shatter. A sound sweeter than any music.

The Bluford Series

Lost and Found
A Matter of Trust
Secrets in the Shadows
Someone to Love Me
The Bully
The Gun
Until We Meet Again

Blood Is Thicker
Brothers in Arms
Summer of Secrets
The Fallen
Shattered
Search for Safety

The Townsend Library

The Adventures of
    Huckleberry Finn
The Adventures of
    Tom Sawyer
The Beasts of Tarzan
Black Beauty
The Call of the Wild
Dracula
Ethan Frome
Everyday Heroes
Facing Addiction:
    Three True Stories
Frankenstein and
    Dr. Jekyll & Mr. Hyde
The Gods of Mars
Great Expectations
Great Stories of Suspense
    & Adventure
Gulliver's Travels
Incidents in the Life of a
    Slave Girl
It Couldn't Happen to Me:
    Three True Stories
    of Teenage Moms
Jane Eyre
The Jungle Book
The Last of the Mohicans
Laughter and Chills:
    Seven Great Stories
Letters My Mother Never Read

The Merry Adventures of
    Robin Hood
Narrative of the Life of
    Frederick Douglass
The Odyssey
The Prince and the Pauper
The Princess of Mars
Reading Changed My Life!
    Three True Stories
The Red Badge of Courage
The Return of the Native
The Return of Tarzan
Silas Marner
Sister Carrie
The Story of Blima:
    A Holocaust Survivor
Surviving Abuse:
    Four True Stories
Swiss Family Robinson
A Tale of Two Cities
Tarzan of the Apes
Ten Real-Life Stories
Treasure Island
Uncle Tom's Cabin
Up from Slavery:
    An Autobiography
The Warlord of Mars
White Fang
The Wind in the Willows
The Wizard of Oz

**For more information,
visit www.townsendpress.com**